Mosaic

By Jo Bannister

MOSAIC
STRIVING WITH GODS
A CACTUS GARDEN
THE WINTER PLAIN
THE MATRIX

Mosaic

JO BANNISTER

PUBLISHED FOR THE CRIME CLUB BY

DOUBLEDAY & COMPANY, INC.

GARDEN CITY, NEW YORK

1987

All of the characters in this book
are fictitious, and any resemblance
to actual persons, living or dead,
is purely coincidental.

Library of Congress Cataloging-in-Publication Data

Bannister, Jo.
Mosaic.

I. Title.
PR6052.A497M6   1987   823'.914   86–16551
ISBN 0-385-23797-9

And if any mischief follow, then thou shalt give life for life, eye for eye, tooth for tooth, hand for hand, foot for foot, burning for burning, wound for wound, strife for strife.

The Book of the Covenant,
as told to Moses: *Exodus* 21

Mosaic law

Mosaic

Burning for Burning

1

The big man with the white moustache like a Viking's leaned in and out of Joel Grant's field of vision. That field was narrowed by the restraints upon him and by his own weakness, but when the big man leaned close he said things and when he moved away he did things, and what he did made Grant scream and his exhausted body twist and writhe like a jerked marionette.

This long after Grant could not remember what he had said, only what he had wanted; nor could he remember what the man had done to him that had hurt so much. Forgetting was necessary, Nature's way of ensuring that he would not spend the rest of his life on the rack, remembering the experience all his waking hours and helplessly reliving it every night. But Grant resented the loss, even mourned it, feeling—though he could not have explained the feeling—that part of his being had been stolen from him. He knew that he had suffered, and survived, but having no cogent memory of the first he could not ever quite focus the second into reality. He dwelt in a kind of limbo, as if the big man had retained his soul.

Nor did forgetting allow him a dreamless sleep. As the big man with the white moustache loomed in and out of his vision he screamed and writhed, and shouted obscenities until someone struck him in the face. The blow was not vicious, not painful, but it was repeated rhythmically and insistently until he began to emerge from the nightmare.

He woke finally to a brilliance of electric light, the slick of sweat down his body, a tangle of sheets about his legs and a sound like the wind that was his own gasping, panting breath. A warm ache of terror lay upon his limbs and his cheek tingled.

A woman knelt on the bed beside him. Her night attire consisted of a wristwatch, and she was mopping his face and throat and the hollows under his collarbones with a cold wet flannel. When she saw intelligence creeping into his staring, terrified eyes she put the flannel into his hand and looked at her watch.

"You took your time coming out of that one."

From somewhere Grant managed to find a shaky grin. "Why leave when you're enjoying yourself?"

Liz Fallon smiled back. "You're getting your sense of humour back."

"No. I'm just getting better at pretending I have one."

She shrugged. "Have it your own way." She did a lot for him that most people would not consider part of a normal relationship, but she drew the line at coaxing him at four o'clock in the morning. There was a pocket diary on the table by the bed. She made a note in it.

Weakness whining in his voice, Grant said petulantly, "I don't see what good you think that does, either."

Liz thought about how he must feel, not only being nursed like a sick child but needing it, and hung onto her patience. "It proves you're getting better. It used to be seven nights a week. Now it's three. That's a big improvement."

"It's still seven," growled Grant, wiping the flannel down his forearms with distaste and hands that were not steady. The sweat had poured from him like a river: even the sheets were damp. "I only wake you up three nights a week."

"You used to wake me up seven, so it's still progress."

"Maybe it's your insomnia that's getting better," Grant said snidely. "There's nothing like good works for a clear conscience."

Liz put the diary back and regarded him calmly. "Joel, do we have to have this conversation now? It's the middle of the night: I'm tired, I want to go back to bed. You should get some more sleep, too."

He mumbled something into the flannel.

"What?"

"I said, I daren't," he shouted. "I daren't go to sleep, because when I do he does it to me again, what he did before, and I can't even remember what it was."

It was not that her patience snapped, only that she recognized when it could do more harm than good. "It's your dream, Joel," she said sharply. "Fight him for it. Hurt him. Maybe if you can beat him you'll be free of it. You were a fighter: well, fight now."

She rose from the bed with serpentine grace, her long golden back smoothly straightening, and walked from his room without haste or hesitation, closing the door behind her with a crisp, quiet, very final snap.

After she had gone Grant went on looking at the light bulb above him until the element printed tiny bright horseshoes all over his retinae. "Fight?" he mused bitterly. "Don't you know, girl, that's the first thing they do to you—knock all the fight out?"

The big man with the white moustache made a small, deliberate gesture of his hand towards the door.

The man on the kitchen chair could barely see the door—that also was deliberate—but the whites of his eyes showed as he tried automatically to follow the gesture. The man on the chair was afraid. He was also black, and here being a seated black man in the presence of a standing white man was enough to make anyone afraid. There was nothing he could do about it, however, except endure it as best he could and show it as little as possible.

De Witte was speaking. He had an unusually deep voice, with a hint of bass music in the lower register which gave range to the customarily rather nasal accent. He also spoke slowly, but nothing about him suggested a correspondingly slow intellect. He might conceivably have got the job other than on merit—a donkey could get elected prime minister as long as it was white and brayed in a Boer accent—he might even have got the reputation some other way. But the hard bright diamonds that served De Witte as eyes could only have been acquired either by mining or by being a cold, clever, ruthless bastard. De Witte's hands were too clean for a miner's; though only in that one respect.

He said, in his deep unhurried musical voice, "That's the way out. You go out that door and you're in a corridor; turn left, round the corner and there's another door, and that one lets you onto the street. It can't be more than twenty strides—the sort of distance you could do in a few seconds from a standing start. But I've got to tell you, boy, you'd never make it. Three ways you can get out of here: dead, mad and co-operative. The last is not only the easiest, it's the quickest.

"Listen, you're not a fool, I'm not a fool, so we won't talk nonsense. I won't tell you that every man who comes in here gives me what I want in the end, because that isn't true and you know it. But you also know that those men who hold out, you don't bump into them on street corners afterwards. You want any kind of life after this, you'll co-operate. You've still got six, seven years on Robben Island, but in the end you'll walk away. It sure beats twenty years in a padded cell or going out the door in a plastic bag. This is not a nice place, you don't want to spend the rest of your life here."

The man on the chair made a tiny shuddering movement. It might have been a spasm of pure fear, except that De Witte, who had seen it before, knew otherwise. It was the fractional muscular tremor of action no sooner decided upon than abandoned. In his mind, and at the end of his nerves, the prisoner had made a desperate dive for the half-seen door behind him; but at the last moment his courage had failed him. Beneath the white moustache De Witte smiled to himself. The first battle was over and won. The man no longer saw himself as a fighter but as a captive. Now that was out of the way, real progress could begin.

De Witte strolled over to the door and leaned against it, casually, letting the lesson sink in. He moved as he spoke: unhurriedly, but with the promise of speed and of strength. He went on: "I understand your position. You've got appearances to keep up. You can't talk too soon. Some things you can't tell me at all. You can't talk until I hurt you some. Don't worry, I know the routine—I've done this before. So what we do is, I'll give you something to show for your visit—nothing too bad, it'll look worse than it is —and then you can give me something to show for my time. It doesn't have to be too important, just something for the files. Then we can call it a day."

Though there's always tomorrow, thought De Witte, a shade bleakly, and the day after that, and the day after that, and pretty soon you'll run out of trivial things to tell me to stop the hurting that will be anything but token, and you'll tell me everything you know and some things you can only guess at before I decide I've had my money's worth out of you. And when we haul in a couple of dozen of your comrades in consequence, they'll come spitting fire and swearing vengeance on your poor tattered hide; but by the time they too have been through this room, and betrayed some friends of their own and learnt to spew up their own insides at the sound of a footstep outside the door, they won't hate you any more. They won't even hate me. They won't have the guts.

Not until late that evening did the side-door he had described open to allow De Witte onto the street. It was a back street, dark and quiet, linking nowhere with nowhere else, where no one came and no one passed, which was exactly how the men who had chosen the site and designed the building wanted it. It was made for secret arrivals and departures. De Witte did not care who saw him come or go, but at the end of a long day it was easier to have his car meet him here than go right through the building to the front steps and meet it there.

Increasingly De Witte found the days long, the work tiring. He wondered sometimes, waiting wearily in the dark for his car, if age was finally catching up on him. He was fifty-nine, a strong and vigorous man, and his command of the business of counter-terrorism had never been fuller, defter or more effective. Only sometimes he wondered if the energy and enthusiasm he invested in the job were as great now as they had once been.

It had to be age. Certainly he felt no less passionate a commitment to the defence of his country. He considered himself fortunate to have been able to serve that passion, in one capacity or another, all his adult life. He was proud of his contribution; not boastful, but quietly satisfied with his record of service to his people and his land. He knew, as no one else could, the number of times his instincts and his professionalism had averted disaster. It was a cause for pride. He also knew what the wider world thought of him: not only black Africa but the querulous white liberals of Europe and America. He could contemplate their self-righteous disapproval with absolute equanimity, even at the end of a long day. There were only four million people in all the world whose opinions he cared about, and all of them were South Africans and all of them were white.

A small sound reached him from across the dark road. There were doorways there too, also belonging to government offices, though the doors were never used: De Witte could not remember when he last saw someone come or go through one. They were no more than black alcoves off the dark street, but in one of them tonight something was crying. It was a tiny sound, barely audible, and he could not be sure if it was a child or a woman, or even an animal in pain. He peered into the shadows. "Hey there: you got trouble?"

The sound stopped abruptly. Then it began again: a faint keening. De Witte, frowning, looked up the street. His car was just nosing round the corner, fifty metres away. What he ought to do depended on who it could be. Not a ter—you couldn't get that sort of sound out of them by nailing them to the wall—so although caution was a necessary part of his life-style De Witte did not feel threatened. He could call the police, in which case some hungry child or woman who'd got herself in trouble would find herself going through the official mill with very likely a charge at the end of it. He could wait for his driver; but he did not care to be dependent on a servant for any more than his contracted work. Or he could do nothing. But he was not an uncaring man. He did his job, and did it thoroughly, because he cared so much about certain things, not because he cared too little. While the car was still half a street away he crossed over, following the thin threads of sound until he found the huddled shape in one of the doorways from which they issued.

It was a woman, swathed in a tattered dress whose print pattern grew clearer in the lights of the approaching car and a rag of a shawl. Her head was also swathed and he could not see her face. He touched her with his toe. "Hey, poppy, you wanting something?"

The glint of eyes put her black face in perspective and she shuffled hurriedly to her feet. She did not look towards the car. She said, "I got what I want," and both the words and the tone were so at variance with the abject manner of her that De Witte straightened, instantly on his guard. But as he stepped back she went with him, her step as elastic as a cat's, and polished metal winked between them in the headlamps' gleam; for only a moment. Then the blade the woman had snatched from her ragged clothes was hilt-deep in De Witte's chest, the woman was lithely running and De Witte was slowly, slowly falling.

He was not aware of hitting the ground, but an incalculable time later he opened his eyes on an oblique view of the dark and dusty street punctuated, somewhat surrealistically, by the white-wall tyres of his car and the shiny boots of his chauffeur. Detachedly, he considered the possibility that Jacob made a better job of boots than any servant in Pretoria. As a kind of afterthought he wondered if a man with a knife stuck in his chest should be worrying about shoes. The knife did not actually hurt; or if it did, it hurt so much that shock was preventing him from registering it. He knew more about the relationship of shock to pain than most doctors, he thought sagely. It was part of his job.

None of this showed in his face. Jacob Sithole, bending over the body of the man who was his employer and thought himself his master, saw only the large still body lying stiffly, almost primly, on its side, the slack face ashy-white in the wash of the headlights, the brilliant-cut diamond eyes half open, vacant and fading. He had to bend close enough to hear the rattle of breath in De Witte's throat to know that he was alive. He looked up the empty street after the vanished woman.

"Oh you bad bastard man," he murmured, more to himself than to De Witte. "So finally you hurt somebody who found a way of hurting you back. So now I guess you think I'm going to bust my gut getting some kind of help for you. For why? So you can get well and hurt some more people? Man, man—you ask a lot."

He gazed down at the man on the ground, and up the street to where there were lights and people and telephones. He began, almost reluctantly to walk. After a pace or two he began to run.

While the big man with the white moustache lay in a hospital room, battling with the pain of healing

which seemed to him far worse than that of the injury itself, and wondering if he should tell Jacob that
his soliloquy had been overheard, his doctor was
serving coffee in his office to Elinor De Witte and
trying to explain why, although the repair operation
had been wholly successful and her husband appeared to be making a good recovery, there was in
fact little doubt but that she would soon be his
widow.

"The knife wound is no longer the problem," he
said. "Though the point actually entered the heart,
the damage really wasn't that great: granted that we
got to him before he bled to death. But while we
were in there stitching him up, we found other problems. Elinor, I don't know how he's kept up the pace
as long as he has. He should have been in here talking
to me three years ago. Then I could have told him:
slow down, take holidays, enjoy your life and your
heart will do you till you're eighty. Now? There's
nothing I can tell him, or you, except that he has the
heart of a sick old man.

"If he gets over this, as he should, and if he never
does another day's work, he could enjoy reasonable
health for maybe ten years. But if he goes back to his
job—any job, really, but his job in particular—Elinor,
he'll be dead in a matter of months. I'm sorry, there is
no gentler way of putting it, we might as well have
the cards face up from the start. He has to choose
between being an old man twenty years before his
time, or acting his age and dying.

"If he'll let us, we can give him a life worth looking
forward to. But that's the choice he'll have to make,
and you and I both know him too well, Elinor, to
suppose he'll choose as we'd wish him to."

Elinor De Witte sat for a long time in the comfort-
able, very slightly shabby surroundings of her own
drawing-room. The familiarity of her belongings,
which waymarked her life with Joachim De Witte
through three decades, was of more support to her
than a close family. She looked at the curios and the
photographs, and when a swift velot dusk swallowed
the golden afternoon it did not matter that the room
was dark because she knew everything in it inti-
mately.

She thought about Joachim: the fierce red lion of a
man he had been in his twenties, defending his land
with his gun and the strength of his arm and his
determination. In those days South Africa was a land
of sun and blood, and a man was judged on his ability
to hold what was his. In their determination to hold
and prosper men like Joachim De Witte dragged the
country out of the tribal morning into the full day of
nationhood. Now their youth was gone and they
were still holding it with strength and determination,
and sometimes also with guns, because the young
men who should have taken their place had not the
same vision, the sense of purpose.

But of all the strong men, and they were all better
known than De Witte, both at home and abroad,
none had made as great a contribution to the survival
of the Republic. A nation under siege, from within
and without, depends utterly on the quality of its
intelligence, and De Witte had created an intelligence service that was the grudging envy of half the
world.

And it was because of his massive importance to his
country, and not because of his incalculable worth to
her, that Elinor De Witte was even contemplating
what she was. It was a thing too terrible to undertake
from even the most loving selfishness.

She had essayed the idea—tentatively, covertly—with Joachim's doctor. He had ruled it out, kindly but totally. De Witte was a rare D-type, he said, explaining what that meant: that the chances of finding a suitable match in the time that Joachim had left were so vastly remote that she should dismiss the possibility from her mind.

Except that Elinor knew something which the doctor did not, something that even Joachim did not know—and which he must never know, whatever she did and whatever the consequences. In the dark room, surrounded by the shadowy pictures her thought-blind eyes needed no help to see, she wrestled with the appalling dilemma her twenty-five-year-old secret had become. She dared not seek help or advice. Anyone capable of advising her in this would have a vested interest, and if she shared her secret with those who needed De Witte even more than she did it would be too late for tears, too late for conscience: the terrible thing would be done. Only while she kept silent could she choose to do nothing; but through the long black night the aching within her pushed her steadily, and at last unresistingly, towards that ultimate act of love and betrayal, and when the clear pale light of dawn crept into the quiet room, from which the agony and the turmoil were finally gone, she picked up the telephone.

2

The man who was De Witte's deputy was unable to fill the big man's shoes. Danny Vanderbilt, regarding him woodenly across the acacia expanse of the desk, was conscious for the first time of the actual size of the office, the size of the furniture, most of all the size of the vacancy left by the man by whom and around whom the department had been constructed. But he nodded politely enough in the gaps left by what Botha was saying. He knew that his opinion was not being sought.

Nor was his discretion being trusted very far, which was another change. If Botha found himself running the department permanently, which God forbid, he would have to learn to confide in his operatives. He had got all this need-to-know nonsense from the Americans he was so taken with, but Vanderbilt saw nothing in the results obtained by the CIA to justify emulating their methods.

"All you need to know," said Botha, and Vanderbilt nodded politely, "is that Colonel De Witte is depending on you finding the man whose file you have there and bringing him in."

Vanderbilt lifted the cardboard cover and considered the photograph. The face was unfamiliar to him. "Who is he?"

"He's a ter," said Botha. He seldom used a proper word if a colloquialism would do. "Listen, I've got better things to do with my day than telling you what you can read. The information's all there: study it. There should be enough there to put you on his track. Find him and bring him in."

That easy, hey? thought Vanderbilt. Aloud he said, "What if he's out of the country?"

A little yellow fire sparked in Botha's jaundiced eye. "He *is* out of the country. He got out, or more accurately was got out, via Rhodesia"—Ian Smith may have capitulated but there would be no Zimbabwe in Walter Botha's lifetime—"five weeks after the Mpani raid and near as we can make out a scant ten minutes ahead of the Army. He went to England. Will you read the damned file?"

Vanderbilt gave a soft low whistle. Impressed in spite of himself, he leafed through the flimsy sheets. "So he was one of the six."

In a celebrated incident two years previously a terror gang had shot its way into the building where they were now talking, killing two security men and a secretary, and released seventeen prisoners from the detention cells in the basement. As most of those detained were suspected associates of Joshua Mpani the raid was widely believed to have been instigated by him, a rumour which was never refuted by the rebel group or its leader. It would probably have been claimed as a victory of considerable propaganda and practical value had the escape proved as successful as the raid.

But De Witte, spitting tacks, had saturated the borderlands with army patrols and put the squeeze on communities known to be sympathetic to the Mpani group. Eight of the seventeen detainees were recovered, another three were killed resisting arrest; fourteen terrorists were taken prisoner, five terrorists were killed. Joshua Mpani was one of them. Six men rescued from government detention reached the safety of the border, but to all intents and purposes it had cost an entire rebel unit to get them there. One of those expensive men was Joel Grant.

"If he's still in England," said Vanderbilt thoughtfully, still skimming through the papers, "how am I supposed to get him out?"

Botha sniffed and jerked his chair forward in a petulant little gesture meant to convey to his subordinate that the audience was over. "You're an experienced man, Vanderbilt. It says so on your record, presumably to explain the ludicrous salary we pay you. You'll think of something."

Vanderbilt elevated a sardonic eyebrow but de-

clined to chase the hare. Sticking stubbornly to the
point he said, "Can I hurt him?"

Botha rocked a hand ambivalently. "So long as you
don't actually injure him. That is important."

Great, thought Vanderbilt sourly. "Then can I—?"

Botha cut him off, inadvertently answering the
question he had forestalled. "All I ask," he said, "is
that you don't involve the embassy."

Two days later Danny Vanderbilt was driving a hired
car up a wet road, shivering intermittently in his too
light clothing, reflecting on the amazingly dismal nature of the main highway linking the city of London
with its chief international airport. He had been here
once before, more than ten years before, and he had
thought the same thing then. Also, it was still raining.

He had a single, slender lead: an address. It was not
Joel Grant's address. There was no reason to suppose
that he had ever been there, or even knew the
woman Vanderbilt was looking for. The connection
was that tenuous.

Two years before Joshua Mpani had a lieutenant
called Nathan Shola. Shola had been one of the leaders of the raid, and one of those to evade the subsequent army dragnet. He was known to have been
with Grant later in Zimbabwe; both had needed hospital treatment, although Shola's injuries had been
superficial. After the black man was discharged they
were not seen together again, and Pretoria had lost
track of Shola's movements. There was no record of
him following, or preceding, Grant to England. But a
girl of Shola's had found her way to England, and was
dancing in the chorus of a strip-club in Soho. She had
been recognized by a businessman visiting London,
whose loyalty to the army he had until recently
served in outweighed any personal reluctance he

might have felt to admit frequenting black strip shows. The address of the club was Vanderbilt's lead, although he had some shopping to do before going there.

Although the grey February day was already drawing in among the high narrow streets of the capital, by the clock it was hardly more than mid-afternoon and Vanderbilt had expected a wait of some hours before he could see the girl Suzanne. But the door of the club was open, a dark gap like a missing tooth beside a shop-window full of marginally pornographic photographs curling at the edges, and the outrageous old queen in the box-office was doing a steady trade in a desultory kind of way.

Vanderbilt paid his way in, grinning to himself at the thought of Botha's face when he came to initial the expense account. Nondescripting his accent—a much more effective and less suspicious vocal dissemblance than assuming someone else's—he remarked through the box-office grill, "I haven't been in London for ages. You still got Suzanne here?"

From close to the old queen was anything but outrageous. He was a rather sad, weary-looking man of more than middle age, in gaudy trashy clothes that did nothing to disguise an essential greyness of the spirit. He was about as gay as a public execution. He hardly looked up at Vanderbilt's enquiry. "Suzy Lavalle? Yes, she's still here. She's on in a few minutes. You want to see her after?"

It was a pleasant change for Vanderbilt to have someone doing his work for him. "That would be nice. You don't think she'll mind?"

The man behind the grille looked up then, with a brief glint of sad humour. "No, dearie, I don't think she'll mind."

She was a coloured girl, and her name was not

Lavalle but Kop. She took him to her room, which was round the corner from the strip-club, and the walk was short enough and the girl uninterested enough that he did not have to do much more than smile and nod from when the old queen introduced them until after the girl locked the door of her room behind them and switched on a two-bar electric fire. "You got a name, honey?" she asked, not looking round as she unbelted her coat.

"You could call me boss," suggested Vanderbilt.

She looked at him then, eyes saucering whitely. There was nothing you could do to a white South African accent that a black South African would stay fooled for long. Anyway it was time for her to know. There were occasions when pussy-footing round got you what you wanted, but this was not one of them. To tell him what he wanted to know Suzanne Lavalle, née Suzy Kop, would have to be very frightened indeed, and she might as well start now.

Vanderbilt left forty minutes later, alone, quietly locking the door behind him. In due course, he supposed, when she did not return to work, somebody might get irritated enough (rather than concerned enough) to force the door. But there had been no noise to annoy the neighbours, even had they been normally alert neighbours rather than the deaf, dumb and blind variety preferred by hookers, and Miss Lavalle would not be capable of making herself heard for some hours yet. Vanderbilt thought he was probably in the clear until morning, and even then he was not worried about official complications. Wherever she turned when she recovered sufficiently to tackle the five pairs of nylon tights presently securing her to the bedstead, it would not be the police.

She might try to contact Shola, if she was thinking

straight enough by then. Or she might find it harder than he would. She had been unable to give Vanderbilt either a telephone number or an address, only the name Shola used in England and the name of a Mickey Mouse newspaper up north for which he occasionally wrote. She was not in contact with him; she had seen him only once in this country, when he got her a job with an African charity. She gave it up after a couple of months: the strip-club paid more, and was more fun. She had heard of Joel Grant but had never met him; she did not know he was in England too.

Vanderbilt was not interested in her life-story, though he did wonder in passing what it was about her that could have appealed to a man of Nathan Shola's physical, intellectual and political prowess; not appreciating that for such a man a fondness for silly women might be less a weakness than a strength. But just now all that interested Vanderbilt was how little she could do about protecting, or even warning, Shola. The most she could do, if she would not go to the police, was call the newspaper and ask them not to give out any information about him, which an English newspaper probably would not have done anyway. That did not matter: Vanderbilt had no intentions of asking for it. By the time Kop was able to contact the paper, he expected to have everything it was capable of yielding.

He returned to his car and searched out the signs for the M1.

Liz Fallon found herself lying awake, with no knowledge of what had wakened her. She was well enough used to broken nights, her sleep fractured by another person's dreams, but that was different, and familiar. After fourteen months the signal pattern of his moan-

ing, tiny animal whimpers growing over a period of
two or three minutes to full-throated yells if she did
not get to him first, was to her as routine a call to duty
as, for example, the pipping of his bleeper to a doctor
or the howl of a siren to a factory worker. She had
installed the baby alarm so that she could wake him
before he reached screaming pitch. Grant had not
liked it but she had made no effort to mollify him. She
made it a matter of policy not to protect him from
life's little harshnesses, only from the big one.

She lay still in the dark room, breathing softly,
listening to silence. Whatever had disturbed her was
not repeated. The half-expected litany of despair had
not yet begun. If Grant was having nightmares, he
was keeping them to himself.

But something prevented her resuming her interrupted sleep: an echo in her mind like a distant
shriek, insubstantial as windsong but insistent, incapable of being ignored. Its very remoteness, its lack
of identity, called to her like a lost child so that at last,
grudgingly but without any real option, she pushed
the quilt off her legs and went to investigate. She
started with Grant, even though what she had almost
heard had not sounded like him, because he was her
charge.

His light was on, a ribbon of brightness under his
door. He must have heard it too, she reasoned, entering without a knock from force of habit alone.

She saw Joel Grant sprawled on the floor, a jumble
of bare arms and pyjama legs, his dark hair tumbled
in his white face, and a big man in a raincoat bending
over him.

Danny Vanderbilt had not allowed for the baby
alarm. It was a rogue card. He had had one enormous
piece of luck tonight, finding the address he had acquired for Nathan Shola occupied not by that large,

tough and sneaky warrior but by the altogether easier target he had intended Shola to lead him to—not
voluntarily, Vanderbilt was an optimist but not a fool,
but perhaps inadvertently, or perhaps there might
have been old letters lying about the house—so it
would be unreasonable of him to resent the unfore-
seeable reverse which had now brought him face to
face with the other tenant of the house.

He knew she was there, of course. He had estab-
lished which rooms were in use before entering the
building, and his first act on the inside was to find out
who was using them. In the master bedroom the faint
beam of his burglar's torch picked out the girl, sleeping deeply and rhythmically, on her stomach with
the quilt slipped down to her waist. Neither the
creak of the door nor the glow of the torch disturbed
her; she looked set to sleep until morning.

In the other bedroom a man was sleeping, fitfully,
the sheet tangled about his legs. Vanderbilt knew it
was not Shola, even in the dark the skin was the
wrong colour, but with his face half buried in the
pillow Vanderbilt could not see who he was. He
thought it did not matter: if Shola was not in the
house the person he wanted to talk to was the girl.
This was her place: her name was over the bell, her
mail was on the hall table, her tights were drying
over the bath. If Shola used it as a forwarding address, she would know where he was. Vanderbilt's
only interest in the man was to ensure that he did not
interfere while she was telling him.

He moved over to the bed, weighing up how to hit
him efficiently from the awkward angle, and as he
stood there the sleeping man moaned and twisted
onto his back. A bar of moonlight admitted by the
imperfectly drawn curtains fell across his face and
diagonally down his body. His body was pocked with

small marks Vanderbilt had seen before. Startled, he looked at the man's face and he had seen that before too. A flash of the torch confirmed it.

"Well, I'm damned," murmured Vanderbilt.

Joel Grant woke with a cry. It was instinct that woke him rather than Vanderbilt's looming presence, his spying torch or his startled, whispered words: an instinct for danger whetted by three years in the bush and honed to a painful edge by two months under interrogation. The big man with the white moustache had sent for him often in the night but never once had he needed to be roused. The footsteps outside, the turn of the lock, had torn him bodily from sleep and left him waiting achingly in a corner with his legs drawn up to his chest, even when he could not stand from exhaustion. Those stretched seconds between hearing their feet and feeling their hands were almost the worst of the whole bad time; at least, so far as he could remember.

Weeks in a Harare hospital had healed his body and the subsequent months in Liz Fallon's house had gone a long way towards repairing his mind, but that instinct for danger went deeper than iodine and kindness and when the conditions which had fostered it recurred—this long after, this far away—that instinct galvanized him like an electric shock and he woke with the cry that Liz heard through her own slumber.

For Grant it was as if the nightmare had finally claimed him back: waking had not freed him from it, left it to slither away, noisome but harmless like seaweed from the ankles of a paddling child, but had confirmed it in its own reality. It was as if he had known of this possibility all along, and that was what the dread was really about: not something that was over but something still to come. In that moment of waking he thought that, by some means which he had not at present the intellectual control to consider, he was back in South Africa, in the security building in Pretoria, in his midnight cell, and the soft background susurrous of despair fell to a breathless pause while booted feet stalked the corridors and the tumblers fell in a single lock. Even through his own surging fear Grant had felt the wash of relief across the rest of the block. He could not blame them for that: he too had known the brief, intense pulse of joy when it was someone else's turn.

But now after two years it was his again, and he jacked himself up the bed to cower against the wall, his knees drawn up to his chest. If any lingering rationality was aware that the fresh stripes over his knees, the cool of cotton sheets and the sophisticated geometric wallpaper half seen by moonshine failed to support his perception of events, the discrepancy did not penetrate sufficiently far into his fear to make him question. Yet some detached portion of his mind, or perhaps only a reflex of his body, knew where he was because while he crouched against the wall one hand was scrabbling wildly for the light switch.

When he found it the room sprang into bright relief. Grant still did not know where he was: the room was not his old cell and the big man looming over him had no moustache, but that was the only difference—he was the same sort of man, his eyes held the same sort of promise, and Grant knew that when he spoke the same Boer accent would lance through his nerves. He did not think he could bear for it to start again.

Vanderbilt had thought he was groping for a weapon. He dived at the crouching man, one big hand pinning Grant's arm to the wall, the other clamping across his mouth. His bones were not much bigger than a girl's, though squarer. When the light came on, almost simultaneously, Vanderbilt realized there was no weapon and allowed himself a pause— kneeling on the bed, the smaller man immobile in his broad hands—to assess the situation. Had they made enough noise to waken the girl? He thought back and decided they had not—a decision in which he was more misled than mistaken. He had still to get Grant out of the house and away without arousing pursuit. For that he had to take the girl out of the equation, at least temporarily. He could gag her while she slept and then tie her without causing her harm, he thought. What he had had to do to the Kop girl still rankled with him. He regarded Grant pensively. He was light enough to carry without inconvenience as far as the car he had left in deep shadow in an adja- cent side-street. This late no one should see them, but if Vanderbilt took his time he could anyway make it look as if he was helping a drunk. Vanderbilt often took risks, but none he did not have to.

Grant's eyes, wide with terror, gazed whitely back over the silencing hand. Vanderbilt made up his mind. He jerked Grant's head forward and then back against the wall, hard, and when his eyes rolled up he tugged him forward onto the bony prominence of a waiting knee which met his jaw with a dull sound like rocks and stopped him dead. Grant's spare body went as limp as rags. Vanderbilt spilled him onto the floor, rubbing ruefully at his knee.

The door opened and a tall naked girl stood golden against the darkness. She looked at Grant's sprawled body. She did not scream or try to run. She said, quite calmly, "Have you killed him?" She was English.

Vanderbilt said, "No."

Even in the one word she caught his accent. She

nodded to herself, as if it proved something. "Are you going to?"

"No. I just want to talk to him."

"You could have talked to him on the telephone."

"I don't somehow think he'd have talked back."

Liz looked at him, insensible on the carpet. His head had tipped back and his throat looked exposed and vulnerable. The marks of his captivity were prominent in the electric light. "You had him for two months in Pretoria and he didn't talk then. What makes you think he'll talk to you now?"

Vanderbilt looked curiously from one to the other, the naked young woman to the unconscious young man. "Did he tell you he didn't talk?"

Liz shook her head. "He can't remember. Others were there. They knew."

Vanderbilt shrugged. "They all say that afterwards. To cover for one another. But most of them co-operate in the end. He did."

Liz Fallon did not care, one way or the other. And because she did not care she knew that he was lying. She smiled. She knelt by Grant's head and fingered the hair out of his eyes. He did not stir. She said to Vanderbilt, "Sure. And some of De Witte's best friends are black communist homosexuals."

She woke five hours later, to the sound of policemen breaking in her door, and she was alone in the house.

3

The Lancashire town of Sorley, where Liz Fallon lived with her lover when he was at home and her good cause whether or not, was undergoing one of its periodic wet spells. This was real northern rain: not

Irish "softness" or the dreary grey drizzle that passes
for rain in London and those parts. When it rained in
Sorley it hit the corrugated tin roofs of a thousand
outhouses with a batter like concentrated machine-
gun fire; it ricocheted up off the worn and settled
flagstones so that a black umbrella was only half the
answer. It yammered at the windows and pooled on
the sandstone doorsteps, in the dips left by genera-
tions of cold stamping feet. And when it rained in
Sorley, it kept it up for days.

The *Western Democrat* was not a Sorley newspaper
for Sorley people. That function was filled by the
much larger *Sorley Chronicle,* which carried photographs of local weddings on the front page and blow-
by-blow accounts of local council meetings and foot-
ball matches inside. The *Democrat,* with its ancient
Cossar press and grainy cliché-block pictures, was
specifically the organ of the immigrant communities
of the north-west, so that while its circulation was a
fraction that of the *Chronicle* its reach was rather
broader: as far as Liverpool in the west and Bradford
in the east.

Many of its readers would have been surprised,
and some horrified, to learn that the *Western Democrat* was not the product of an immigrant staff but the
conception, creation and favoured first child of a
young white Englishman with a degree in political
science and a bequest from his grandmother. Will
Hamlin was not twenty-seven, still owner and editor
of the *Western Democrat,* still a champion of immi-
grants' rights and concerns, reluctant but resigned
host to a small well-behaved ulcer, and employer of
one journalist, three printers and Nancy Prescott, the
jewel in his crown.

Nancy was engaged as a secretary, paid as a personal assistant and mostly occupied in riding shotgun

on a stable of contributors whose articles were invariably pertinent, controversial, committed and late. Nancy Prescott was also white, but never more so than this morning when she opened up the office and found what had happened to it in the few short hours she had borrowed to go home and sleep in.

Ten minutes after Nancy opened the door on mayhem, Will Hamlin came clattering up the uncarpeted wooden stairs behind her. He had left the place even later than Nancy the previous night, and it showed. He stood dripping amid the debris of emptied drawers and scattered papers, his shoulders slumped. Under his sodden hair his face was set and grim, but his eyes were hollow with shock and a kind of grief. Nancy did not know how to console him. She said, "The police are coming."

Hamlin nodded, absently. He was an intelligent, articulate man, capable of great eloquence and argument that was both impassioned and of impeccable reasoning, and all he could think to say of the rape of his enterprise was, "Why?"

The detective who arrived not long after was able to provide answers of a sort. "Well, it wasn't vandalism. Someone may have it in for you but not in that way."

Hamlin spread a hand helplessly at the mess. "But —what good—?"

"He was looking for something. It may look random; actually it's anything but. He's emptied every drawer, every file, every cupboard in the minimum time possible. Whatever he was looking for, either he found it or it wasn't here."

"There's nothing—valuable—here."

The policeman shrugged. "That may depend on how you define valuable. Mr. Hamlin, this was a professional search. There was nothing casual about it.

He knew what he was looking for, and he knew how to look, and I'm inclined to believe he also knew where to look. All these papers—presumably they tell you something?"

"Records," said Hamlin, bewildered. "Mostly records—advertising accounts, correspondence, VAT. Last week's copy. Some back material I haven't found slots for yet. Nothing."

"Something," the policeman demurred, "we just don't know what yet. How long before you can say if there's anything missing?"

Hamlin looked at the paper mountain in the middle of his floor. He looked at Nancy, at his watch, at the ceiling, finally at the detective. "When is it you retire?" he asked gently.

The police had done almost all they usefully could and were preparing to leave when the telephone rang. Hamlin answered it. He listened, almost in silence, for a long time. Then he lowered the handset, offering it rather vaguely to the CID sergeant. "It's the Metropolitan Police." He looked appalled.

Amazement sent the sergeant's eyebrows and the pitch of his voice soaring. "For me?"

"Not exactly. But I think you'd better hear what they have to say."

Behind Vanderbilt as he drove Grant lay unconscious on the floor of the hired car. Had he been going further he would have stopped somewhere dark and lonely enough to transfer his passenger to the boot: it was a big car with a capacious boot, Vanderbilt had had this contingency in mind when he chose it. But he wanted to be off the road by dawn, and judging by past experience he did not expect Grant to be up to causing problems before then. He drove, fast but carefully, away from Sorley and towards the naked backbone of England. Where the road crossed into Yorkshire it began to climb in earnest and the succession of small towns gave way first to villages, then to isolated farms on windy hills, finally to the expansive moors of the Pennines themselves. There was no traffic, either on the main road or when Vanderbilt veered off onto the B-routes, and only the occasional glimmer of a distant light where a farmer was calving a cow or burning some other agricultural midnight oil.

When the shapes of trees began to show up against the lightening sky, Vanderbilt began looking for somewhere to hole up. It was not the work of moments because his requirements were precise. He wanted an empty building—vacant house would be ideal, a disused barn would do—where he could secure his prisoner and stay out of sight until he could arrange their passage home. The route had already been prepared and primed: one phone call and within a few hours he would be on his way.

Three times he investigated apparently disused laneways only to be turned back by eventual signs of continuing occupation. Once a dog rushed at the car, barking, but no lights sprang up in the dark house it guarded; still, Vanderbilt drove a long way before he tried again.

The fourth cart-track he essayed crept between overgrown hedges and plunged down a steep hill before washing up against the stony outcrop of a labourer's cottage. It was long and low, built like the rock of ages, and weeds and brambles pressed silently at the door, craving an admittance that would not be denied much longer. In the laneway tall grasses bowed gracefully to the bumper of the car.

Vanderbilt turned off the engine and sat for a moment with the window down, listening and watching

the house by the beam of his headlamps. There was
no sound, no movement: everything about the look
and feel of the place suggested it was abandoned. At
the end of a minute he got out and went to the front
door and knocked. When there was still no response
he walked round, wading in places through growth
thigh-high, until he found the side-door, which he
broke down with a bull-buffalo shove of his shoulder.
He went inside quickly then, moving from room to
room. The house was empty.

He moved the car round the back, out of sight from
the laneway—not because he expected anyone to
come calling but because he had reached the upper
echelons of a perilous profession by being very, very
careful—and carried inside his holdall and the body
of Joel Grant. Grant was still deeply unconscious: his
hands danced slackly on limp wrists in time with
Vanderbilt's stride and tapped against the backs of
his legs when he stepped over the threshold.

The house appeared less neglected from the inside
than the outside. The roof was sound, there was no
damp; there was a smell of must but not of mould; the
glazing was intact. There was no electricity, but after
a reluctant movement and with a tinny shudder of
protest cold water ran from the taps. The rooms were
sparsely furnished: a dining-table but no chairs, a
settee and an oak dresser downstairs, beds and big
solid wardrobes in the upstairs rooms. Almost nothing was left that could have been removed easily: no
cutlery, no pots, no bedding, no curtains. Someone
had died here, Vanderbilt surmised, and after the
relieved relatives had taken everything they conve-
niently could the house was closed up to await a
purchaser who never came. Vanderbilt looked out
from the dusty window at the grim hills pressing
round, shading lighter now from black to battleship

grey, and knew that he had come to the right place. This cottage had served as a prison before.

He carried Grant upstairs, bothered more by the narrowness of the stair than by the weight, and deposited him on one of the beds—that in the main bedroom, which was the most solidly framed. There was no point tying him down to something that a couple of good shakes would pull apart.

The holdall contained items he had bought in London before proceeding to Soho. They were things he had not wanted to bring through British Customs, things the average tourist or businessman would have had difficulty explaining away: not so much the torch, the comprehensive maps, even the commando knife, which might be justified by a somewhat unseasonal camping expedition, as the bottle of sedative and the hypodermic syringes, the spare passports, the electronic gismo that was a radio beacon and the large quantities of sterling. He hoped not to need the passports, however, and whatever money he spent would have to be fully accounted for to Botha.

There were handcuffs, too, which he used to secure Grant to the iron bedstead, and a blanket with which he covered him. Vanderbilt had not taken the time to dress him before leaving the house in Sorley, so he was still in his pyjama trousers and the raincoat Vanderbilt had bundled round him to make him less conspicuous for the short walk to the car. The pale sun was barely proud of the hill and the house had been cold for a long time, and Vanderbilt assumed that if Botha did not want Joel Grant harmed he probably did not want him with double pneumonia either.

Before leaving—he hoped and expected this would be the only time he would have to leave Grant

until after they arrived in Pretoria—he thumbed
Grant's eyes open and shone the torch in each of
them in turn. Nothing moved there, and Vanderbilt
saw no prospect of him waking in the half-hour he
would be gone. He frowned over a quick mental
sum. Grant had been unconscious two hours already
and showed no signs of returning yet. Vanderbilt suspected he may have hit him too hard. Even with
experience, it was difficult to assess the degree of
force which would render an opponent incapable of
slogging back without putting him on the critical list.
Vanderbilt was not really worried; but if there was no
change when he got back, he would begin to worry.

He drove back to the last village they had come
through which had a public telephone.

Despite the dull ringing in her head, Liz Fallon began making sense before either the police or Will
Hamlin did. To be fair, the investigating officer,
whose name was George Corner and who would
have been a hairdresser instead had he anticipated
the juvenile glee with which successive colleagues
would dub him Corner of the Yard, was probably
more concerned at this stage with being reassuring
rather than honest; but Hamlin, who had spent most
of his adult life writing about the rape of human
freedom, was genuinely shocked numb by this unexpected personal attack.

After the police had gone, and the doctor summoned by the police had gone, and the ambulance
summoned by the doctor had been turned away by
Liz who was recovering quickly enough to be getting
angry, she sat Hamlin down with a mug of coffee
heavily laced with whisky. He murmured something
about the milk being off. She smiled and nodded and
topped up his mug, and at length he looked at her

rather more intelligently and said, "I don't actually know you, do I?"

"You were here for Nathan's party. Eighteen months ago, when he got back from Africa. I was the one passing the biscuits."

Hamlin nodded but vaguely; clearly he did not remember her. A thought crossed his open face. "Was Grant here then?"

Liz shook her head. The thick rope of her corn-coloured hair danced on the collar of her towelling-robe. By her standards she was prudishly dressed. "Joel was still in hospital in Zimbabwe. Then we had to get his immigration approved. He got here last February. After three weeks of Lancashire winter he was about ready to go back."

Talking about it resurrected the picture in her head of the damaged man Nathan Shola had brought to her. Skeletally gaunt, his angular limbs assuming defensive postures seemingly of an independent will, his skin bleached by months out of the sun, he looked younger than his twenty-three years; except for his eyes, which were dark coals burning fever-bright with bitterness and resentment in the deep pits above his prominent cheekbones. His eyes were old with horror and hatred. His hands shook slightly all the time. It was impossible to imagine how he had appeared before his three months in hospital.

Nathan Shola introduced them, then added quietly, "My friend needs some help."

And she had helped him: partly because Nathan asked her to, partly because Grant was a casualty in a cause she respected, mostly because by the time she realized the scale of the task she had taken on Joel Grant was no longer a task but a person. She cared about him and what became of him. It was not love. She was not drawn to him in that way, although on

occasions she had lain with him when his need was so
great that only her close strength stopped the black
heart of his mind from breaking out and engulfing
him. It meant no more to him than it did to her; less,
she believed, because she did not think he liked her
as much as she liked him; or perhaps it was only that
needing put a greater strain on a relationship than
being needed.

The anger waxed in her. He needed her now. If he
had regained consciousness, if he were still alive,
wherever he was he would be needing her as ur-
gently as he ever had. Caught up in the resurgent
nightmare, he would grope for her in his personal
darkness and she would not be there; scream for her,
and she would not come. He was alone in his worst
imaginings.

"Damn them," she cried aloud, "haven't they done
enough to him?"

She had already called Amsterdam. Nathan Shola
would be on the first plane home. Now it occurred to
her to wonder if that was what the Boer wanted. She
said to Will Hamlin, "After all this time, what can
they possibly want with him?" Hamlin shrugged
wretchedly. Liz laid a hand on his arm as he sat
hunched on the settee beside her. "No, listen, this
could be important. Could it possibly be a trap for
Nathan?"

Hamlin looked horrified but he thought about it.
Then he shook his head. "No."

"Why not?"

He mumbled into his chest, "Wrong bait."

When she realized what he meant, Liz knew he
was right. "Yes. It would have been as easy to take me
as Joel. Then why?"

"Revenge? They were badly embarrassed by the
Mpani raid."

"If it was only that they could have killed him and left him here. It would have served the same purpose and been much safer. You don't need to kidnap a man to make an example of him."

"Perhaps they still want information from him."

"After two years? What could he possibly know that would still be relevant? Your paper's more up to date than that."

Hamlin managed a rueful grin. "What did he say to you?"

"The Boer? Just that he wanted to talk to Joel."

Hamlin was unconvinced. "You were unconscious for hours. He could have talked to him here. You can hurt someone a lot in quite a short time if there's nobody to interfere. Instead he ran the risk of being seen carrying or dragging Grant out of the house and presumably into a car. He must have had a good reason for that; a strong, important reason."

A chill like fingers ran down Liz's spine. She felt herself pale. "You don't suppose for a minute they'd try to take him back to Pretoria, to talk to him there?"

Danny Vanderbilt watched Joel Grant wake. He had been unconscious a long time, but then Vanderbilt had hit him hard and had made no subsequent efforts to coax him back into the land of the living. Contrary to what he had told the girl before hitting her—the white girl, not the dancer—he was not remotely interested in talking to Grant. As far as he was concerned, the later he slept the better. It was going to be a long day.

A roll of carpet underfelt against the bedroom wall made a tolerable seat. With his large square chin resting on his forearms across his knees, Vanderbilt watched his prisoner struggle towards the light and wondered what it was about him that seemed familiar.

Grant's head in the shaggy halo of a homespun haircut, moved restively between his pinioned arms. His breath came in small laboured grunts between parted teeth. A frown had grown between his brows that was screwing his eyes against the day. With his wrists lashed to the bedhead, the fingers laxly twitching and clenching, and one knee drawn up, he seemed to be giving birth to his own awareness.

When his head stopped rolling and his grunting breath softened to a shallow panting, Vanderbilt saw that his eyes had opened a crack and were sliding, vague and unfocused, across the spartan room. He stood up and moved closer to the bed. Grant's weightless skimming gaze touched on him and stopped. His eyes opened wide with shock before closing on a gathering despair. A faint moan whispered through his dry lips.

"That's right, sonny," Vanderbilt said quietly. "You didn't dream me."

From the capacious holdall he produced a carton of milk and a packet of biscuits. He freed Grant's left hand so that he could feed himself. "Behave yourself and I won't tie you down again."

Grant weakly invited him to participate in an act of self-abuse as impractical as it was obscene. His eyes flinched with the expectation of pain, but Vanderbilt only grinned.

"That's all right. You don't have to like me. All you have to do is obey me, and you really can't do anything else."

The knowledge that he was right soured the milk in Grant's belly; only an effort of will kept him from throwing up.

With his senses returning to him like a flight of

weary pigeons, one at a time and in no particular order, Grant did not know where he was, how he had got there, how much time had passed or what was likely to happen next. But he always knew who was responsible: not Vanderbilt personally, but those behind him. He had known in the brief waking seconds before the Boer floored him back in his own room in Liz Fallon's house, and he had known with the first crack of awareness that stirred in his battered brain as he lay tied to a stripped bed in a grey and dusty room he had never seen before. He knew it was Pretoria; mainly because nobody else would be sufficiently interested to spit on him if he was burning, but also because of the craven twitching of all his nerve-endings. The people in Pretoria had put a lot of time and effort into teaching him to fear them, and now his body responded to their implicit presence like a trained dog. Deaf and blind he would know them, and shake like he was shaking now.

Vanderbilt saw him shivering and casually tossed him his coat. Grant fielded it with his free hand and hurled it back, fear and fury blazing in his eyes. Vanderbilt calmly moved his head out of the way and let the coat fall harmlessly to the boards. He shrugged. "Suit yourself."

"Why don't you get on with it?" shouted Grant. His own accent, keener than always, scraped across his nerves like a rasp.

"With what?"

"What you came here for. You want something, don't you? From me. So get on with it. It's quiet enough for you here, isn't it? I can yell my bloody head off and nobody'll come running. Damn near as good as Pretoria, hey?" The words rushed from him like a torrent from a glacier, fast and urgent, frenetic, beyond control or containment. His face was white with shock, graven with deep lines and stained with black under both eyes and along the line of his left jaw. Gaunt, raging and wrapped in a blanket, he looked like a mad prophet. Vanderbilt thought he might have to hit him again to shut him up.

"Damn you," shouted Joel Grant, *"listen* to me!"

Vanderbilt's gaze, which had wandered, came back to him with the force of a slap. "No, you listen to me, because already I can tell that quite a small amount of you is going to get right up my superior maxillary sinus. This may come as a disappointment, but I don't want anything from you. I'm not interested in anything you know: not enough to plug your fingers into the wall socket, not enough to feed lighted cigarettes to your bodily orifices, not even enough to ask nicely. That may be somebody's job, but it isn't mine. As far as you're concerned, sonny, what I am is a kind of Universal Aunt. I'm here to make sure you get home safely."

The wind poured off the Pennine fells. It soughed through the hedges and round the corners of the stone house, and its voice was the voice of bleak centuries. Half a world away the sun was warm, the autumn breeze laced with the garden scents of bougainvillea and frangipani, the equinox hanging in the heavy air like an electric promise. With the new rains the young land would spurt into growth; the whole lovely country would smell like a garden.

Except for the bits that smelled like a charnel house. Joel Grant stopped shivering long enough to meet Vanderbilt's eyes. The ghosts in his white face added up to a kind of resolve. He shook his head. "Only in a long box."

4

Will Hamlin met the flight from Amsterdam. Even in
the hurrying, shuffling crush of Customs he had no
difficulty spotting Nathan Shola. The African was
high, black and handsome, a slender two-metre warrior in a business suit. A handgrip was all his luggage,
and he held it aloft and hip-swerved his way towards
the exit like an attenuated rugby player heading for
touch. He flashed brief brilliant smiles to smooth his
passage, but his eyes and all his attention were on the
barrier. He was looking for Liz; but Liz had wanted
to stay by the phone. Hamlin's larger, solider figure
caught his attention as he made a second scan.
    "Will?"
    "Nathan. This way, I've a car outside." They shook
hands without break in pace. "You made good time."
    "Over the Scheldt I got out and rushed. Will, what
the hell is going on?"
    Driving back to Sorley, Hamlin repeated all he
knew, including everything Liz had told him and
everything the police had said about Suzanne
Lavalle.
    Shola swore. His long tensile body carried about it,
like a charge, an aura of latent, almost urbane, sav-
agery that invested plain words with unexpected violence. In consequence he seldom spoke viciously:
"damn" was about as rough as his language ever got.
"Is she all right?"
    "She will be. Though I gather it may be a while
before anyone pays to see her with her clothes off."
    Shola's mobile, sculpted lip curled. He made a
mental entry in his personal Book of the Dead. "And
Liz?"

"Liz has a bump on the head, that's all. She's fine. No," he corrected himself—he tended to sub-edit his conversation as he did his copy—"she's scared for him. And very angry."

Shola grinned tightly. "That sounds like Liz." The smile died. "But it was me he was looking for—me he asked Suzy about?"

"Probably only as a way of tracing Grant. He didn't know where to look for him, but he guessed Suzanne would know where to look for you. Presumably he thought he could get Grant's whereabouts out of you." Hamlin shrugged apologetically. "Well, Suzanne didn't know where you were, but she knew you wrote for the *Democrat* and the name you write under. He knew I'd have an address for you. I imagine if I'd been working late last night I'd have been in for a hammering too. As it was he raided the files and came up with Liz's address. Then he went round to ask you where Grant was; only you weren't in the house and Grant was. He struck lucky."

"He couldn't have taken Joel as a bargaining piece?"

Hamlin shook his head. His eyes never left the road, which in view of the speed at which he was driving was probably just as well. "He'd have taken Liz, Nathan. Besides, he never asked her about you. He wasn't interested in you. He'd got what he came for."

Anger and frustration were mounting in Shola like a head of steam. His voice quivered with mayhem but did not rise. "But why? What can Joel tell them? Mpani's dead, our people scattered—anything he could tell them now would be two years out of date. Even if he talked."

"Perhaps," suggested Hamlin, "they don't need him to talk. Perhaps they only need him to be there."

"Pretoria?"

"Yes. Suppose that what they want is to take him back and put him on trial. Nathan, he's a white South African who sided with black guerrillas against his own kind. He fought for the Nationalists, and when he got caught they fought for him. Maybe that makes him some kind of a symbol. Maybe it has become politically necessary for the government to get him back, break him and put him on show. Is that possible, do you think?"

"In my country anything is possible." Nathan Shola let out a long breath like a sigh. "Poor Joel. My poor, poor friend."

Liz was out of the door and down the steps before the car stopped, and before Shola was properly out she had flung herself at him, grafting herself to his long body like a liana embracing a forest tree. "Oh Christ, Nat," she gasped breathlessly into his neck, "I'm glad you're here."

Together they hurried inside.

Chief Inspector George Corner was not idle. By midmorning he had wired copies of Grant's photograph to ports and airports throughout the country, to mainline railway stations and to the Metropolitan Police; had circulated with it a good description of Vanderbilt and had arranged for a police artist to visit Liz Fallon's house; had been in touch with Special Branch, fully briefed his superiors and prepared preliminary reports for those government departments which would become involved if Joel Grant did not turn up safe and well in a very short space of time. Then he had a cup of tea and tried to remain civil in the face of a new station sergeant who had just now discovered the humourous potential of his chief inspector's name and was wetting himself behind the filing cabinet.

Vanderbilt had achieved a modest comfort beside the bedroom window and was doing his job with such supreme efficiency that he did not appear to be doing it at all. Without moving his head, just by flicking his eyes, he could take in the track, or at least its course between the hedges, almost as far up as the road, or check his prisoner. Joel Grant, one wrist still shackled to the bedstead, was curled up foetally on the mattress as if wrapped round a hurt.

Vanderbilt was confident that no one would approach the cottage by the natural route without giving him time to act. At the first sign of movement in the lane he would drug Grant and release him; if the owners of the cottage turned up to evict him he would go, taking his junkie friend with him, and no one would take them for other than social outcasts using a squat. Only if a serious attempt was made to detain them, which probably meant a policeman, did Vanderbilt intend using violence.

But he anticipated no such problems, any more than he expected the cottage to be rushed from the back. In all likelihood he would leave here with Grant towards the end of this same day without anyone being any the wiser; but even if someone saw them there was nothing to connect them with the incident in Sorley. Possibly three days from now, when some bright policeman had all the pieces on his desk, he might put them together—the kidnapping, the cottage that was used as a refuge, the helicopter that landed briefly on the fell at dusk and the abandoned hire car found by a shepherd next morning— but by then Vanderbilt would be safely back in his own country, and Grant . . . well, whatever.

Vanderbilt was a professional, which meant that by and large he concerned himself with the hows and left the whys to other people. He did not know why Pretoria wanted Grant back now, after so long, and he did not very much care. He knew the order came from higher up than Botha so he was fairly confident that there was a good reason: his government did not risk confrontation with those few other governments that were less than overtly hostile merely on a whim.

He would have been happier still if the job had been handed down by De Witte, in whom he and his colleagues had an unshakable faith, but he knew that De Witte was, for the present at least, sidelined. There was even talk that the old bastard was dying. Vanderbilt, who had seen him in the hospital after the knifing, remained to be convinced. He did not think that the colonel was anything like ready to swap certain power in the here-and-now for doubtful authority in the hereafter; but perhaps he would not be offered the choice. It was like a man saying that if there were blacks in heaven he would not go. If it turned out there were blacks in heaven, neither De Witte nor Vanderbilt nor most of their compatriots would be invited.

Vanderbilt shrugged inside. He had long ago come to the conclusion that if God was capable of knowing everything a man had done, He should also be able to divine his motives. He did not consider himself, or any of them, evil men, only men charged with the almost superhuman task of keeping entropy at bay and given only flawed tools to work with. There were aspects of South African affairs he was not overly fond of himself, but he did not see anything demonstrably finer or fairer when he looked to the governments of his country's black neighbours. There seemed to be something in the African soil that begot violence and butchery: that beautiful, vibrant, bloody land. The only choice for white South Africans was between riding the tiger and dismounting.

Outside the cobweb-curtained window the fell was grey and brown, the wind was cold, the sky was low and heavy with the threat of more rain. The only sign of life as far as the eye could see was a sprinkle of white on the far hillside, and Vanderbilt knew that no matter how long he watched no sudden explosion of tawny power, no fleet and spotted courser with the long legs and serpentine body of a greyhound, no tireless pace of pied nomads would come to set the sheep in dizzy motion. Danny Vanderbilt suffered a sharp pang of homesickness. He did not want to be here; and if he thought about it, though it was generally wiser not to, he did not much want to be doing what he was doing here—dragging a bound and frightened boy back to one kind of death or another in a Pretoria basement.

Grant was shivering more violently than before. When the links chaining him were just barely touching they rang out tinily, like a miniature tattoo or a distant tambourine, the meter of his tremors. Vanderbilt wondered if he was really sick—wondered, indeed, how anyone stayed healthy in such a climate —and why Botha had put that unusual emphasis on preserving his prisoner's well-being. He left the window and quietly walked over to the bed, picking up the flung coat as he passed.

Grant appeared to be sleeping. His sunk eyes were all but closed, only a thin white line showing under each lid, and his breathing was ragged but unchanging. His skin was cold and damp to the touch, his face waxy. Vanderbilt spread the coat over him.

The gentle touch, the weight of the coat, or perhaps only the proximity of the big man wakened him.

He woke with a wordless cry woven of sounds of anger and despair, his unfettered arm flailing. Metal clashed as he snatched repeatedly at the short chain. The wildness of his struggle, like a man trapped in madness or epilepsy, startled Vanderbilt who pressed the writhing man firmly back against the bed, the coat tucked under his chin. Suppressed by hands like sandbags his struggles grew weaker. At length the only movement under the coat was the rapid rise and fall of his chest.

Bending over him, pinning him still, Vanderbilt said grimly, "Sonny, I told you, if I have to I'll tie you down good. This is bloody cold country, you got to keep covered up."

Something odd happened. Vanderbilt was bending over Joel Grant, looking into his face from a range of inches, and then—without warning and just for a moment—it was not Grant he was seeing at all but someone else, someone else's eyes and expression, someone he knew. He snatched a startled breath, his senses groping, but the illusion was already gone, dissolved as quickly as it had formed, leaving the cognitive portion of his brain dry-spinning and his eyes searching Grant's eyes with an intensity that did not reflect what had actually passed between them.

Grant gasped, "You're crazy. You're going to kill me, and you're worrying I might catch cold?"

Vanderbilt straightened up slowly. The phantom recognition had jolted through him, mind and body, like an electric shock. He did not understand what had happened—he was a pragmatic, unimaginative man—and, it disturbed him. He said, "Have I seen you someplace before?"

Grant sat up awkwardly, levering himself up one-handed, pulling the coat about him with a bad grace.

"Were you De Witte's understudy in the black hole of
Pretoria two years ago?"

Vanderbilt acknowledged the description with a
sardonic twitch of the lip. He shook his head. He had
slightly long dark blond hair. "It wasn't there."

Grant's lip curled thinly. "Then it wasn't anywhere, because I remember the other bits of my life
and I don't know you from Adam."

Vanderbilt shrugged and moved back to the window, but he could not shrug off the feeling of unease
which lingered in the wake of his small, unlikely aberration. Outside the sun was higher but nothing else
had changed.

On her way up to her husband's hospital room Elinor
De Witte was waylaid by his doctor and steered
gently into his office. Her heart turned over once and
then went racing with the expectation of tragedy,
but it was not that. Harry Keppler smiled reassur-
ingly as he guided her to a seat; a tray with cups and a
steaming pot was waiting on his desk. She had known
him well for thirty years. She knew what he was
going to say. She wished one of them might die before he said it.

Dr. Keppler poured the coffee confidently with
fine strong hands, not needing to ask how she preferred it, and passed it to her. She put it down quickly
before he should hear her agitation rattling cup
against saucer. Keppler smiled again and laid his cool
hand on her forearm.

"Tomorrow, Elinor; or as soon as the courier can
get here. It's time Joachim was told."

Her skin crawled. The fine hairs along the back of
her neck stood up. It was as if he did not know the
circumstances, that what the courier was bringing
was a living man with a human soul. But of course he

knew, it was relevant medical information, he was just trying to keep it professional and impersonal, to save her feelings. He need not have troubled: she would never feel clean again. She wished he would not touch her.

"I thought you might like to tell him yourself."

"No!" Her hand flew to her throat; she felt the pulse flutter there like the heart of a captive bird. "Harry, don't ask that of me."

He drew his own chair closer and sat down. "You know I won't force you to do anything you don't want. I know how difficult this has been for you—traumatic, even. But think of Joachim. In a few minutes someone is going to go into his room to tell him that in the course of the next twenty-four hours he's going to undergo major surgery with no guarantee of success. He knows the situation: he knows he can die under the knife, in the recovery room, or of any of a thousand complications that can come up without warning over the next several months. Think how he must feel. He needs all the support he can get, and you and I both know that all my professional expertise will mean nothing to him compared with you sitting there holding his hand. Don't you owe him that much?"

She jerked to her feet; the full cup went tumbling from its perch on the arm of her chair and she paid it no heed. "Harry Keppler, don't you presume to tell me what I owe my husband. I *love* my husband; I love him so much I have done a terrible, evil thing to keep him with me. I can't afford to think too much about what I've done, and I can't afford to talk to him about it because I just might tell him the truth.

"Harry, you could count on the fingers of one hand the number of times I've lied to Joachim. The last big lie was twenty years ago, and that was about this boy too. I haven't practised enough to become good at it. If he came to suspect the truth, or even half of it, he'd put a stop to the whole monstrous business, and then I would lose him and so would this country. So if you've any sense, Harry, you'll go in there and tell him yourself, just what you want him to know, and I'll come in afterwards and sit by his bed and hold his hand, and I won't say a word until you come for him. And may God forgive us all."

Nathan Shola spent the morning on the telephone. He made calls to Europe, to America, to various places in Africa and repeatedly to London. From time to time he received calls in return. He was cashing in old favours. By lunchtime he had found a name to go with Liz Fallon's description of the Boer, and had identified him with an élite direct action office run personally by De Witte but for the present by a man called Botha. He knew that Vanderbilt was respected as an effective operative and was credited with two kills outside South Africa. One was a reluctant informant who died under interrogation in a disused tobacco shed in Angola, the other a defector who thought himself safe in Miami under the protection of the FBI.

He had also learned about the attack on De Witte, that the damage had been repaired but that he was still in hospital. He had heard the rumour that the big man was dying anyway, and the other rumour that the hospital was standing by for a last-ditch attempt to save him with a heart transplant. However, Shola's informant discounted this as unlikely: there had been difficulty in locating enough blood of the right type for him after the stabbing, which suggested that the search for a compatible donor organ would probably take longer than a man with a bad heart had got.

"There's something wrong here," Liz said thoughtfully when Shola had finished his report. "I grant you, if they wanted Joel back for a show trial, Vanderbilt is the man they would send and he would go about it pretty much as he has. But is it the kind of operation that would be initiated by De Witte's stand-in? Look at it from his point of view. He's probably wanted the job for years; finally he sees it within his grasp. He knows that a permanent decision will depend largely on how he acts now. So *is* he going to stake his career on an operation as unnecessary and prone to failure as this one? How much prestige is there in the show trial of a sick man when, whatever the court decides, it's bound to result in an international incident?"

Hamlin was nodding. "She's right, Nathan. They can't put him on trial. Grant is a *bona fide* resident here, entitled to the full protection of British law. Pretoria can't admit openly to having sent an operative to kidnap him. The British Government may make a show from time to time of disapproving of the Republic, but by and large relations between them are equable. South Africa hasn't so many friends on the world stage that she would deliberately set out to alienate one. If they do take him back, they'll have to keep him under wraps for the rest of his life and then bury him in an unmarked grave. And what good will that do them?"

Shola indicated agreement with a slow inclination of his narrow head. There was nothing he could add: their reasoning was good. With all their special knowledge of the situation, the more they thought about Joel Grant's kidnapping the less sense it made.

The atmosphere in the small front room had grown thick with breathing and frustration, and with the smell of cold coffee from the several cups shouldering for space on the table. None of them had felt like eating; none of them had felt much like coffee either, but periodically Liz or Will had got up to make some, primarily to occupy their hands. The idea of occupying them with some washing-up never seemed to occur to them. They seemed to have been sitting together in that room for days, not hours. They were all tired.

Shola stood up abruptly, stretching to dislodge the tension and fatigue gathering in his muscles. "Then it is something he knows that they're after."

"And we've already agreed that makes no sense," said Liz, a shade testily.

"Then we were wrong," replied Nathan Shola. "Or more correctly, there's something we don't know about that makes sense of the apparently absurd."

"Perhaps we're assuming too much," offered Hamlin. "Can we be quite sure that this is to do with Grant's guerrilla activities in South Africa?"

Liz blinked at him. Shola stared with frank surprise. "I would have said it was a fairly safe assumption."

Liz said, "What else, for God's sake?"

Hamlin shrugged, apologetically. "Well, how long has he been here? Something over a year? What's he been doing in that time? All I'm saying—asking—is, could he have done something to lay himself open to this kind of counter-attack?"

Liz and Shola exchanged a look heavy with significance. Shola strolled over to the window and lowered himself gracefully onto the sill, crossing his long legs at the ankles. "You haven't met Joel, have you?"

Liz said, "You can forget it, Will. There is no chance of Joel having resumed covert action for his cause in Sorley."

"Would you necessarily know?"

"I would know," she said, "through living with him, and Nathan would know because that's his work —it's his job to know. For now, Will, Joel has enough trouble making it from one day to the next without getting himself involved in revolutionary politics."

"But he was involved," pursued Hamlin. "He cared enough to join Mpani in the first place, and that couldn't have been the easy option. Mightn't he care enough still to follow events, to meet people; conceivably to hear something?—I don't know, something that Pretoria could want to know. Isn't it possible?"

"No," Shola said firmly.

Liz expanded. "You see, Joel was damaged. The damage they did to his body was unpleasant but it healed; those scars don't trouble him much. But the damage they did to his mind won't mend in a few months or a few years. I doubt he'll ever be entirely free of it. It haunts him. He wakes yelling most nights. He hardly leaves the house. He talks to almost nobody but us. If I have friends in, mostly he stays in his room. If we're watching television and somebody with a South African accent comes on he starts to shake. One night last month the police came to the door. A neighbour's kid was missing and they wanted me to check the garden, the shed—you know. After they'd gone I found Joel at the kitchen sink, spewing his guts up."

After a lengthy silence Hamlin cleared his throat and said, "They really messed him up, didn't they?"

Shola spat with a sudden ferocity, "De Witte did. When he was taken—Joel—he knew everything about Mpani. Places, names, dates—everything. We needed time to break it up, get people away, make new camps, new routes. Joel gave us that time, but it took everything he had: all the courage, all the strength. That was why we had to risk everything to get him out. He'd earned it. Even knowing what it cost, he was worth it. I could kill people who judge him by how he is now. That's what they did to him. That's what De Witte did."

"Nathan, I'm not judging," Hamlin said gently. "I'm just trying to think what they could want with him."

Liz said, "He must be frightened out of his wits." Behind her eyes there was a quiet rage.

Nathan Shola said, "I'll find them. And I'll kill the Boer bastard." He made it a promise.

5

By mid-afternoon Joel Grant had just about acknowledged his position as hopeless. He had tried threats, he had tried entreaties, he had even tried bribery although he owned nothing of value and did not know there were people who would pay money to see him safe. But Vanderbilt remained intractable. He seemed faintly amused by both the threats and the bribes.

Curiously, Grant was feeling rather better. He was not as cold, and both the concussion and the shock were wearing off. Even the stark terror that had lacerated his mind like a sharp knife was beginning to dull, the recognition that he was as good as dead already serving as a kind of neural anaesthetic. There was a certain numb comfort in the thought that his situation could hardly get worse.

Vanderbilt had the holdall open on the boards beside him, the electronic gadget that was the radio beacon on his knee. He was familiarizing himself with its operation: it was important that the thing transmit for the minimum period necessary, and he did not want to waste time setting it up or closing it down. He practised until he could do it with his eyes closed.

The beacon was necessary because, for both security and practical reasons, no specific rendezvous between himself and his helicopter had been arranged. When he telephoned in after taking Grant he nominated a broad area within which he would locate a suitable landing spot. In return he was given a frequency for the beacon and the flight path the helicopter would follow. Now he had only to drive to the nominated area and wander round the lanes until he found an appropriate field on the flight path. When he heard the helicopter he would activate the beacon, the machine would home in on him and they would be airborne again within a very few minutes. The beacon would be transmitting for perhaps as little as thirty seconds, on a short-range and little used frequency where there was scant chance of arousing someone's curiosity. It was a system Vanderbilt had used before, always with satisfaction. It was simple, elegant and efficient, and it meant he did not have to commit himself to a meeting-place when all the professionals knew that meetings were the most dangerous part of their work. It was another example of Vanderbilt's extreme, almost pathological, caution. But he did not care that some of his colleagues considered him an old woman. All that concerned him was that when his transport descended out of an overcast sky there should be no one to watch him heave a wriggling sack on board.

Except that the sack would not be wriggling. The sack would be half-way across Europe before it even started to stir. That was what the sedative was for. Grant would be oblivious before he left the cottage.

Vanderbilt did not expect to be stopped on the road but it could happen; there were other reasons for flagging down a car besides suspecting the driver of kidnapping, and Vanderbilt did not want to have to kill an English policeman who stopped him to warn of a defective brake light and heard the boot hammering. Then there was the transfer from the helicopter to the cargo plane waiting at Gatwick. It would be discreet but it would inevitably be seen by someone. The plane was supposed to be waiting for spares: it would be better if the boy did not start yelling.

When he was happy about the beacon, Vanderbilt picked up a syringe and the bottle of clear liquid and read the dosage on the label.

Grant was watching him. "You're not shoving that into me," he said with conviction.

"Good stuff, this," said Vanderbilt, charging the syringe carefully. "You'll be half-way home before you know you've left."

Grant's narrow jaw came up, belligerently. "I thought you needed—" Then a kind of darkness fell behind his eyes. His nostrils flared on a sharp breath and he looked away. "Do what you want. I can't stop you." He had spent the last half-hour trying to conceive of a form of suicide available to a man tied to a bed under the gaze of his warder, and he had almost handed back unused probably the only chance he would be given.

For perhaps a minute it seemed as if the exchange had passed into history without Vanderbilt recognizing its significance. He finished filling the syringe, carefully laid it aside on the windowsill and read again the label on the glass bottle. Then he looked across the room at the man on the bed, and out of his

broad bland face the gaze was as sharply piercing as
thorns. "What did you start to say there?"

Grant stiffened. He tried to relax the taut muscles
but could not. He thought that his rebel body was
intent on betraying him so that it could go on living.
He thought his body must have forgotten what the
price of that betrayal would be. He grunted, "Nothing."

Vanderbilt rose unhurriedly and strolled over to
the bed, and stood over Grant looking down at him
thoughtfully. Automatically Grant moved away from
him; as far as he could, tugging himself up by means
of the handcuffs to crouch against the iron bedhead.
If Vanderbilt started hitting him it would make no
difference whether he was lying, sitting or doing a
tap-dance; if he could not run away he would get
hurt, but some surviving shred of self-respect argued
against waiting for it prone.

But Vanderbilt was not proposing violence, not
yet. He was talking—reasonably, with that same
compound of sweet reason and iron patience that
teachers use on difficult children. "Yes you did—
don't you remember? I said I was going to knock you
out with the hypo and you started to say you thought
I needed something. And then you stopped, because
you thought I was making a mistake and you thought
it could work in your favour. What were you going to
say?"

Grant spat, "Go to hell." He saw his chance of an
easy death beginning to slip away from him. In desperation he decided that a sudden and noisy diver-
sion was his best bet. He hoped that if he turned
suddenly rabid Vanderbilt would shoot the drug into
him without giving the matter any further consideration, to keep him quiet. He also hoped that it would
prove as lethal as he expected: he was not a doctor,

he only knew that drugs they had given him at Harare had almost killed him before they realized how savagely allergic he was to a broad spectrum of their chemical arsenal. Hoping he would not just wake up later and sicker than expected, he launched a low and dirty swing at the looming Boer with his free left hand.

Vanderbilt caught his swinging fist in the palm of one hand, without rancour, and held it with no apparent effort. He went on talking as if nothing had happened. "You aren't exactly wild about going home, are you? So maybe in some way you figured an armful of this stuff would change that. Only one way I can see, but maybe you're scared enough to welcome that. So what you were saying was, you thought I needed you alive. What's the matter, boy, you got allergies?"

"No," muttered Grant, but he could not make it sound convincing.

Vanderbilt grinned at him and released his hand. "Pretoria may have had trouble getting the truth out of you, but I bet they always knew when you were lying."

The undisguised amusement in the big man's tone stung Joel Grant to anger. With a certain terse dignity that would have surprised his friends, he said, "It'll be time enough for you to mock me when somebody's done to you what Pretoria did to me and you've come through it better—boy."

The parting shot was an obvious and deliberate insult, intended and taken as such. Vanderbilt swung instinctively; instinctively Grant flinched away from the broad hand; but at the last possible moment the Boer amended the blow from a punitive slash across the face to an almost friendly swipe across the top of the head, the sort of tap you might give a presumptuous child. Grant was left cringing for nothing: as the anticipation of assault ebbed he felt a tide of humiliation rising through his hollow cheeks.

Vanderbilt watched his discomfiture with half a smile, like a man enjoying a sly joke. But behind the smile, in the place where he did his thinking, he was troubled. If Grant had begged him not to use the drug he would have gone ahead with a clear conscience, confident that the only thing Grant was allergic to was the thought of having to pay for his treachery. He knew that once that needle slid into his vein any hope he might have had of contriving an escape was gone. He did not know his captor, could not know that anyway there would be no chances because Vanderbilt never took any. He must consider that his liberty, and ultimately his survival for he clearly believed that going home would cost him his life—and for all Vanderbilt knew to the contrary he could be right—depended on staying awake now.

But he had not pleaded for his awareness. He had almost said nothing; so nearly nothing that the significance of the swallowed comment could easily have been missed or misunderstood. Vanderbilt was not blind to the possibility that Grant was double-bluffing him—that it was a lie which Grant wanted him to believe, so that having sown the suspicion a feigned attempt to cover it was the best way of ensuring its germination—but there were two objections. The first was that Grant hardly seemed up to that degree of subtlety, and the second that the ground bait was insufficient to guarantee a bite. He was inclined to believe that Grant both thought and hoped the drug would kill him.

There remained the strong possibility that Grant himself was mistaken—perhaps not about his medical condition but about the effect this particular drug would have on it. Pretoria had had him for weeks: plenty long enough for any problem which threatened his successful interrogation to emerge. They would have used drugs; they would know about any hypersensitivity. If Pretoria had given him this compound it was because it was safe. De Witte did not make that kind of mistake.

But maybe Botha did. Vanderbilt did not know. He decided to back his instincts, his skill and his luck, and hold off drugging Grant until he was left with no option. He did not expect it to come to that. He was confident of his ability to manage his prisoner with one hand tied behind his back, whereas in fact the reverse would be the case. There was some risk involved, but there was risk anyway and he had come too far and gone to too much trouble to go home with a corpse.

The decision made, he delayed no longer. He repacked the bag, though he left out the loaded syringe which he put, its needle carefully capped, into a deep pocket of his coat. He unlocked the end of the handcuffs he had fastened to the bedstead, and in a rough parody of dressing a child he pushed Grant's arms into the sleeves of his raincoat. Grant tried to pull away from him but Vanderbilt tugged him back, without difficulty or rancour, and joined his hands behind him. Then he turned him round and buttoned him up with a grin. "What is it they say here?— That should stop you catching your death."

With his bag in one hand and the short chain linking Grant's wrists in the other, towing him backwards through the still house, he made a last tour of the upstairs windows, checking all the angles before he made his move. There was nothing to see: even the distant sheep had wandered to another part of the fell. Except as prompted by the wind, nothing stirred in the overhung lane at the front.

He found himself listening to the house. Its age disconcerted him. He supposed it was a few hundred years old, and unless someone took a bulldozer to it to make room for a motorway it would probably last another few hundred. His country was not as old as this little ordinary stone house; and unless he made a serious on-the-job blunder one day he rather expected to live long enough to witness its demise. The thought caused him sorrow but not despair: he was a practical man, he knew nothing was forever. Not Rome, not Camelot, not South Africa.

But in the meantime he had his work to do, from which not even the gentle remonstrance of the silent house could deflect him. When the time came for Vanderbilt to quit he would do it properly, honourably, face to face over a superior's desk. He would not cut and run in the middle of a job, however distasteful, however convenient . . . With a snort of internal laughter Danny Vanderbilt pushed his prisoner towards the stairs, aware that he was paying too much heed to the sententious ramblings of a silent old house.

Joel Grant was also contemplating the age of the house. It had been built at a time when the needs and wishes of the owner rather than the contents of the Town and Country Planning Act dictated the design, and from the way the roof timbers swept down low over the top of the stairs, the first owner was clearly a short man. Vanderbilt, on the other hand, was a tall man. He would of course stoop under the low beam; unless something distracted his attention at the critical moment. Grant, amazed to feel the old dynamic stirring in his veins at the prospect of action, tugged

petulantly at his bonds until the Boer tightened his
grip on them. Then he launched himself into space.

Afterwards Vanderbilt could hardly believe how
completely he was taken aback by the manoeuvre.
He was watching for trouble outside, had largely
written Grant off as a source of anything more than
irritation; even so he could have dealt with the unexpected or explosion of effort if he had not misinter-
preted its meaning at the very start. Because of what
had gone before, his initial thought—the only one he
had time for—was that Grant was still intent on suicide. Rather than let him plummet to his death of a
broken neck at the foot of the stairs he hung grimly
onto the chain linking Grant's wrists and let the iner-
tia of his big body act as an anchor.

Before the anchor could bite and hold, however,
Vanderbilt had been jerked forward the half metre
that was enough to bring his head into sharp contact
with the beam. Sick pain burgeoned behind his eyes
and he felt his knees go weak; in a jumble that was
mostly legs the two men piled down the narrow stair-
case with Vanderbilt on top. Grant collected more
bruises, and for a wrenching moment as he brought
the Boer's weight down on him he thought his shoulders had dislocated, but foreknowledge enabled him
to protect his head and when they hit the floor he
recovered faster. He kicked and squirmed his way
out from under and rolled over one raging shoulder
to his feet. Vanderbilt was groping for his senses:
Grant kicked him twice in the face to make the
search harder—barefoot he made less impression
than he might have hoped but the second kick rock-
eted Vanderbilt's skull against the thick panel of a
sturdy hall cupboard with a satisfying dull report.

Grant waited no longer but took to his heels. The
bolt on the back door delayed him only a moment

and then he was out into the freedom of an English afternoon. Adrenalin surged in his blood like champagne, but in the bubbles was a renaissance of the fear which had by and large abandoned him when his cause seemed beyond saving. Now he had regained some measure of control over his fate he was terrified of losing it again. He bolted, like a hare, for high ground, past the car and up the green lane that led to the road. Oblivious of the gouging stones under his feet, he did not know he was leaving a blood spore.

At the top of the lane he paused briefly, bent over his heaving chest, then turned left. He did not know where the cottage lay or where he might find help. He knew he needed people: not one or two, that a man like Vanderbilt would kill cheerfully to cover his tracks, but dozens—a village, a pub, a full bus. He chose left because that way the road fell, whereas to the right it went on climbing—a distinction that mattered not at all to a man in a car but meant everything to one on foot.

Remembering the car warned him of the certainty of pursuit. He did not believe he had put Vanderbilt out of commission for more than a scant few minutes: long before any prospect of help drove up this lonely upland road, Vanderbilt would. Even if he turned the wrong way—if he was dazed enough not to guess that a tired man would want to run downhill—he would come back after a mile. If he stayed on the road Grant was as good as caught; and caught, as good as dead.

The roadside was lined on both sides with stone walling, most of it topped with barbed wire. When he came, still running, bent almost double with a pain like fire in the muscles of his arms, to a place where the rusty wire had broken and coiled back on itself, he rolled over the wall and dropped into its shadow, pressing his back against the stones and his cheek into the wiry wind-flattened turf.

Almost at once he heard the car.

Vanderbilt was pinching his bleeding nose with one hand, steering with the other. He was not driving fast and his big face, though bloody, was calm. He was not so much angry, even with himself, as absolutely intent on rectifying the situation before it could slide beyond salvage.

He came up the green lane without pausing, because there was no other way for Grant to have gone, and at the top he turned down the hill because he knew the running man would be feeling the cramps of exertion by then. From there on, however, he drove slowly and kept a careful watch. He could not guess if Grant would run until his lungs burst, gambling on finding some help or sanctuary in the few minutes his gambit had bought him, or whether he would go to ground. There was plenty of cover, if a man knew how to use it. Grant would: now he would, now that he had started thinking like a soldier again.

Vanderbilt was aware that he had underestimated Grant. Frightened, hysterical, arguably psychotic, he was still the product of a rigorous military training which owed as little to the Marquis of Queensberry as it did to the Geneva Convention. The fact that he had left all that did not mean that it had left him: in his mind he might have retired to a staid and timid civilian existence, but given the right circumstances his body would always react as a soldier's. Now that Grant knew that too he would be harder to handle. He would also be harder to find.

Vanderbilt drove beyond the furthest point he thought Grant could have reached—he had been badly dazed by the unexpected attack but he had not entirely lost consciousness or an awareness of the passage of time—then turned the car. Then he crept back, studying the fields on both sides, scrutinizing the walls for signs of disturbance and the middle distance for movement. He saw none. On one side there were sheep grazing, their scattered pattern and steady cudding a guarantee that no one had gone that way. On the other side of the road the land fell steeply towards a swift little river swirling brown from recent heavy rain up on the moor.

At intervals of fifty metres Vanderbilt got out of the car and leaned over both walls to check their shadows.

He was almost back at the lane which led to the cottage when, returning to the car from such a sortie, he saw the blood. It was not copious, only a smear he could never have seen from a moving car, but he recognized it at once and knew what it meant. He silenced the car's engine so that he could listen and turned once more down the hill, on foot, scanning the tarmac surface minutely until he found the spoor again.

He followed the faint trail for perhaps sixty metres and then it ended. On one side were the sheep; on the other the stone wall had lost its crown of barbed wire. With a quiet surge of confidence Vanderbilt vaulted over.

He landed knee-deep in old bracken. Brakes of the wet brown stuff spread dense fingers across the slope. If Grant had burrowed deeply into that lot it could take hours to find him, and Vanderbilt did not have hours to spare. He had a rendezvous with a helicopter less than an hour from now, and first he had to find a suitable landing spot. If he did not recapture Grant in the next thirty minutes he would have to spend a second night in this country, with the police using every extra hour to intensify their search, tighten their grip on the airports and call in the expert assistance of men who had met the De Witte machine before. Vanderbilt had counted on getting his captive out before that degree of mobilization could be organized. Tomorrow would be twice as hard as today, and the day after might be impossible. If they got close enough that he felt breath on his neck he would kill his man and get out like a criminal, in his own time and by a devious route; but if he did that he doubted if he would work again. At least not for De Witte; maybe as a free-lance assassin.

He looked down the sodden patchwork field towards the rushing little river and contemplated failure. He could not afford to spend time beating the bracken for a skulking boy he should have had the sense to dope before detaching him from the bedstead. At least if he had died it would have been Pretoria's mistake, not his.

While he thus ruminated on his predicament another portion of his brain, that area where he was a professional first, last and always, was conceiving of a solution. When he had it a small light kindled in his eye, a small cool smile touched his lip and he climbed back onto the road and fetched the car.

He considered shouting a warning but decided it would be ignored. He drove the car into the stone wall, accelerating all the way.

The impact broke the wall into a hundred tumbling rocks that hit the ground, bounced once or twice and hurtled off down the slope, gaining momentum as they went, crashing a broad swathe through the stands of bracken. Vanderbilt hurdled the rubble and set off in pursuit.

The small avalanche was half-way down the slope and beginning to run out of steam, and Vanderbilt was beginning to worry that his tactic had achieved nothing more than a bit of vandalism—or at the other extreme a silent crush of blood and bones in the flattened bracken. Then, with the noise of the stones like hollow thunder about his ears, Grant's nerve broke and he struggled up out of the tangle and jerked round to face the danger.

It was a mistake, but by the time he saw that the nearest of the bounding stones would skip by him harmless metres away Vanderbilt had him marked. The big man slowed almost to a saunter behind the dying avalanche. He knew that, chained, Grant could not run anywhere that he could not be over-hauled in a few strides. Grant knew it too. Vanderbilt thought the panic was over. He smiled from under his nosebleed. "There you are."

Joel Grant felt a scream building up inside him. It was like in Pretoria, listening to the footsteps stop outside his door; or maybe worse because of the sanity, the normality, the safety all around. Things like this did not happen in England.

But it was not altogether like Pretoria. In the corridors of small rooms under De Witte's office there was no freedom, not of body, mind or soul; none of the freedoms that separate life from existence, not even the freedom to die. On this wet northern hillside, though his snatched liberty was restricted in both space and time by the big man bearing down on him, a kind of hope remained. The mounting scream erupted not as sound but as sudden, galvanic movement as he broke for the river.

Vanderbilt raised his voice in complaint. "Grant, for pity's sake! I can catch you as easily that side of the river as this, only then we'll both be wet." Reluctantly he changed up a gear, jog-trotting after the running man.

There was a shallows where the brown water

raced spumy over a spit of rock. Grant ran past it, leaping recklessly downstream along the rugged, uneven bank where the river turned dark and fast, hurrying unbroken over the deep smooth bed.

Vanderbilt frowned, wondering why. Then he knew why and he was running too, harder than Grant, the big muscles driving his thick legs like pistons, his broad hands seeming to grapple the air out of his path. There was nothing graceful or fluent about the way he ran; sheer strength gave him speed. He was a scant dozen yards behind when Grant threw a last, fast glance over his shoulder—in a split second Vanderbilt recognized hatred, fear, resolve and a terrible grim triumph: a compound nothing short of madness—and then he was gone. The river received him with hardly a splash.

For a brief moment trapped air ballooned the fabric of his coat towards the surface. Then it escaped in a silent silver explosion and the dark thing that was the man was rolled down into the turbid race.

Grant made no attempt to find his feet. He had no interest in the far shore. The surging little river, which was even in the deeper reaches just shallow enough to wade breast-high, was plenty deep enough for his purposes. With enough determination a man can drown in a gutter. As he felt the cold current take him he emptied his lungs of the buoyant air and filled his mouth with water. He could taste the acid peat. But for the most fiercely ingrained of human taboos with which the body frustrates the will, he would have breathed it deeply into him, such was his haste to die. His tumbling body collided softly with the muddy bed of the stream and he was rolled along it with relentless energy by the hurrying flood. If he had wanted to he could not have saved himself then.

Vanderbilt, who had no desire to die, paused on the bank just long enough to rid himself of his heavy outer clothing and his shoes. He waded into the icy brown flood some way downstream from where Grant had disappeared. The cold gnawing at his groin made him hiss; under his breath, while he groped through the water, he whispered with vicious monotony, cursing Grant in three languages.

The stretched seconds passed. Only a very few of them now marched between Vanderbilt and failure. Twice he dived, his spread fingers sweeping the silted bed, but he could not see through the brown fog and the strong current tugged him away from his station. Each time he recovered his feet with difficulty, setting his big body against the river, trawling it with wide arms, wholly aware that his best efforts could not stop tons of the opaque brown stuff passing him by with every second, enigmatic, any burden it carried hidden from his gaze. With mounting desperation he wondered if he should submit himself to the current, let it bear him away with its other trophies, in the hope that chance might bring him the prize endeavour denied him.

Something touched his leg. It did not feel like a man's body tumbling against him, or anything he could put a name to. But Vanderbilt had not paused to consider what it might be. That flaccid random touch was all he had been waiting for, and at it he flung himself bodily at the thing deep in the water.

For a moment he could not find it; then the frantic, slow-motion milling of his hands connected with something inert in the stream and his fingertips recognized the texture of cloth. Groping for an elusive hold he encountered the gossamer threads of floating hair: he twisted it in a grip that Victoria Falls would not have broken and lunged for the surface and the shore.

But it had taken too long. Vanderbilt could see that as soon as he lifted Grant's face to the surface, and when he hauled the drowned man out onto a little muddy spit where the sheep came to drink he knew for sure that Grant had won. In his thin face, fish-belly white and chill to the touch, the eyes were half open. Nothing moved under the hooded, translucent lids, no breath whistled past the bloodless lips onto Vanderbilt's lowered cheek, and when he ripped the coat buttons open the narrow chest naked beneath was still.

In weariness and frustration, and something else to which he gave no name but which could have been grief, Vanderbilt expended the last of his breath in a small and bitter epitaph. "Damn you, Joel Grant— you better like dead now you got it."

He went to get up and walk away and begin the long, depressing journey home, but his big cold clumsy body was heavy with exhaustion. He pushed himself off Grant with a hand on his bare breast. Under his palm fluttered a tiny movement that struck him momentarily rigid.

Strength came from nowhere. Before he had worked out logically that where a heartbeat lingers death has yet to occur, Vanderbilt had yanked Grant's head back, forced his jaws apart and clamped his mouth on Grant's mouth in a strange parody of a kiss that had everything to do with life and nothing to do with love. Counting in his head, making himself take his time, Vanderbilt pushed big steady draughts of air into Grant's starved lungs. His chest rose under Vanderbilt's chest. He breathed for himself and then again for Grant; and again, and again.

Finally he breathed into Grant's lungs and Grant

responded with a tiny choked cough in his mouth. Gasping, grinning, Vanderbilt rolled him onto his face and let him vomit away the bitter water into the mud. He pressed his hands against the heaving ribs under Grant's bound arms and helped the water out. "Breathe, damn you," he panted, rocking, letting his weight do the work; "damn you, live."

Wound for Wound

1

By the late afternoon, with no news of any kind, the tension in the terraced house had built up to such a pitch that Liz had said she could stand it no longer, she was going out for some fresh air. She took her car. Half an hour later Will Hamlin found the letter Sellotaped to the coffee jar. It was addressed to Nathan Shola. The African read it and then said, very quietly, "She's gone."

"Gone where?"

Shola passed him the letter and Hamlin read.

"There's nothing I can do here," she had written, "except sit by the phone and dread it ringing, and fill my head with crazy pictures. So I'm going to Pretoria. If we're right, and if the police can't find them in time, that's where Joel will end up. He'll need one of us to be there.

"You wouldn't get past Immigration, and though they might let Hamlin in they'd watch wherever he went. They won't follow me. My papers are good, they don't know my name and I'm the right colour. Maybe if I can find out what this is all about we can stop it.

"I won't contact your people there unless and until direct action is the only answer; and I won't call you unless I need your help more than I need my cover.

Don't worry, I won't do anything rash. Mostly all I shall be doing is listening. If Vanderbilt is stopped, or if Joel is dead, I'll come out the same way I'm going in, as a good little tourist. But if they get him as far as Pretoria he's going to need all the help he can get, and then maybe having someone on the spot will somehow make the difference. Anyhow, I feel I have to be there.

"I know you won't do anything crazy, like trying to stop me, or following me. You can do more for Joel's safety, and to some extent for mine, by aiding the search here in England: remember, probably no one in the entire police force knows the Boers like you do.

"If everything works out I'll see you in a few days. Look after yourself; but get the bastard."

Hamlin looked up, startled, when he had finished. "Of course she's wrong. You will stop her."

"No," Shola said very softly.

"Nathan, you must! There's nothing she can do in Pretoria without putting herself at terrible risk."

"That is her choice."

Hamlin did not understand. There was anger in his eyes as he reached for the telephone. "I'm sorry, Nathan, but if you won't call the police I shall. I know Grant's your friend, but—"

Shola's hand closed gently, immovably, over the instrument. "Joel is my friend," he agreed quietly. "He is also Liz's friend. I have no right to tell her what she may do for her friends, and certainly, Will, you have none. She is not our property, even by virtue of friendship. Her life and her time are in her own gift."

"And if she winds up in a South African gaol?"

"She'll be in good company. Most of our friends have served that apprenticeship."

Hamlin stared at him, clearly shocked. "Hellfire, Nathan, it's not the same. She's—"

Shola raised a faintly sardonic eyebrow. "White? Like Joel. English—like you? A woman?" He shook his head, laughing softly. "You people have some primitive ideas; but a great sense of rhythm."

Hamlin yielded up the phone with an explosive, frustrated gesture of his hands. "Then what *are* we going to do?"

"What she said. Fight." Shola thought for a moment, then began to dial, calling the numbers out of his head. "She was right about something else. My people know the Boers: we know who they are and we watch them. There are Boers here too. If the one who has Joel needs help—a plane maybe?—that's where he'll turn. That's our edge, the thing we can do that the police can't—have someone watching all the cats to see which one jumps."

Vanderbilt found a suitable field virtually on the helicopter's flight path. Right on top of the hills, where there were no dwellings and the only roads were mere ribbons of fractured tarmac used exclusively, but still not very often, by farmers and forestry workers, a brake of dark conifers girdled a rough meadow. There had been a cottage there once, the tumbled walls still stood shoulder high, and the few open acres had provided the occupants with a vegetable garden, grazing for the house cow, maybe a handful of sheep. Now it was reverting to moorland, and in a few more years the Ministry of Agriculture would acquire it too, the Forestry Commission would plant it and there would be nothing left to show that people once eked out a kind of living on these hard hills but yielded at last to the temptations of supermarket shopping and church hall bingo.

At the agreed time Vanderbilt turned on the radio beacon; almost at once he heard the faint tinny throb of rotors. The sound grew rapidly but he could not see the machine until it suddenly lifted over the trees, surprisingly close and unexpectedly large. It was flying below radar, following the nap of the land. Vanderbilt switched off the beacon and showed himself. The down draught from the whipping blades cut through his dry suit to his wet body and set him shivering afresh. His overcoat was in the boot of the car.

After a brief pause there was an answering wave from the egg-shaped cabin and the monstrous bee settled towards him, head up. The wind and the proximity of the big skids forced him back a pace. The pilot grinned at him through the big Perspex window. The helicopter was a French job, in the dignified livery of a London business house—an executive runabout for people whose time was vast quantities of money, most of whom would have been horrified to know the use to which it was currently being put. Not because of the South African connection, Vanderbilt reflected sourly, since much of the money that made them worth their own sky taxi came from the mines of his homeland; nor even from outrage at the rape of a man's liberty and all that was likely to follow it—for if Vanderbilt did not know what Pretoria wanted with Grant he was at least fairly sure it was not permitted under the Geneva Convention; but for fear that such activities could lead to disclosures that would knock whole pennies off the price of shares.

The pilot did not belong to that Nelson fellowship. A professional like Vanderbilt, he worked with his eyes open and his hands steady, confident that—even if their actions were often illegal and sometimes immoral—their existence was essential to the prevention of greater evil. If discovered they would keep their mouths shut and their fingers crossed: they would not deny all knowledge and claim to have been hoodwinked. It was a more honest form of mayhem.

Vanderbilt had known the pilot for some years. He had worked with him in Europe and once in America. He knew him only as Piet, and strongly suspected that was not his name. His occupation, which was also his cover, made him especially useful but also involved him in abnormal amounts of documentation. It was easier to hide his real identity from those who knew his involvement with Pretoria than from those on whom he relied for licences.

They exchanged a nodded greeting as the helicopter settled on the rough grass. The vibrant roar of the engine died back and the manic clatter of the rotors subsided to a whisper as they slowed to idle. The pilot swung down from the cockpit, looking round. "I thought you had a passenger for me." His accent was ambivalent. His narrow face sheltered behind a large fair moustache. "If I'd known it was only you I'd have told you to take the train."

"If I'd known it was you flying I'd have walked." Vanderbilt indicated a maroon shadow under the trees at the edge of the field. "Our friend is waiting in the car."

Piet raised a sandy eyebrow. "Is that wise? I mean, how keen can he be to go home?"

"It's funny, that," said Vanderbilt, "he doesn't seem keen at all. However, the boot locks from the outside."

The pilot nodded, moustache twitching with a grin he was trying, not too hard, to suppress. "Been giving you trouble, has he?"

From his greater height Vanderbilt fixed him with a severe eye. His expression did not flicker. "Trouble?"

Piet started to walk with him to the car but Vanderbilt waved him peremptorily to his machine. "About the time I can't secure my own prisoner without help from a sky jockey," he said with dignity, "I shall retire to a corner of the family farm up the Orange River and grow coffee. You get that glorified egg-whisk ready to leave and let me get on with my own job."

The pilot turned back with a grin. As he climbed into the cabin he shouted after Vanderbilt, "I know the Orange River country. It's rubbish."

Vanderbilt grinned too, cheered by the meeting, mostly because it promised a quick end to the excursion but also because talking with a countryman about a place he cared about was a timely reminder of what the excursion, and all the other excursions, were for. Like De Witte, and in the same often bloody ways, he was a patriot. If he did not always like what he did, he valued what he accomplished.

Inside the big boot Vanderbilt's big lightweight coat swaddled the folded, cramped figure of Joel Grant. It was not so much a gesture of humanitarianism by the Boer as a reflection of his mounting irritation: he had been put to too much trouble to take home a corpse, and he was worried that his own sodden coat would leach vital heat from a body already pushed to, and briefly beyond, the limits of endurance.

Grant did not move when the boot lid lifted but he was not dead, or comatose or asleep. His eyes focused on Vanderbilt, but dully, as drained of emotion as his body was sapped of strength. Vanderbilt hauled him out and set him on his feet, and draped the coat

round his bare shoulders like a giant cape, and
pushed him down the field towards the helicopter, its
rotors idling softly in the gathering dusk, and twice
picked him up when he fell.

Piet, going through his pre-flight checks as if he
had not been flying the machine five minutes before,
saw them coming and broke off in surprise. No one
had told him Vanderbilt's prisoner was white. It disturbed something quite fundamental to his equilibrium: like looking at a picture of two white faces that
suddenly turned into a black candlestick and said
meaningful things about one's early life and struggles. In Piet's model of the world terrorists came
exclusively in the shadow shades. But there was
clearly no confusion in Vanderbilt's mind: he had his
man trussed up like a chicken, his hands behind him,
so that when he stumbled he could not save himself.
Twice he measured his length on the wiry turf and
twice Vanderbilt hauled him up, single-handed, like
a bag of groceries.

As they came down to the helicopter a thought
occurred to Vanderbilt. His broad bland face screwed
up in a brief grimace. From inside the cabin Piet
frowned a question mark at him. He shouted a reply,
but the whistling wittering of the circling blades
drowned out his voice. The pilot dropped to the
ground. "What?"

"That electronic gismo," mouthed Vanderbilt. "I
suppose we should take it with us?"

"The beacon? Christ, yes." Piet nodded vigorously.
"They trace where those things are made, they're
getting a little close to home. Where did you leave
it?"

"In the car." Vanderbilt sighed. "Watch him for
me, I'll go get it. No, *watch* him," he added forcefully
as Piet turned back to his machine. "He's sneaky."

The pilot humoured him. "I'll watch, I'll watch."
He smiled: an easy, confident, handsome, invulnerable young man's smile. Vanderbilt wished he could
warn him—not against Grant, who was a spent force,
but against feeling that confident in a line of business
as likely to drop one in it as this was. But Piet, though
younger than Vanderbilt, was still old enough and
experienced enough to know the rules. Perhaps it
took confidence to regularly trust one's life to a machine kept improbably aloft by a screw and a theory.
Thinking that Vanderbilt cast a suspicious glance at
the rotor, but it was way above his head, out of reach
for even an athletic suicide. He turned away and
headed back up the hill. After a moment, largely to
show he could, he broke into a jog.

Joel Grant said, "I'll make it worth your while to
help me." His voice was low and breathy, unenlivened by much hope.

The pilot eyed him with curiosity and dislike. "Get
in."

"They're going to kill me. If that mad bastard gets
me back to Pretoria, they'll kill me slowly."

"I think you're confusing me with someone who
cares."

Grant's head rocked back and he laughed. There
was not, in truth, much humour in it, it had a hollow
graveyard ring, but from a man in his position it was
undeniably impressive. It impressed Piet. It also disguised the fact that Grant was subtly shifting his position relative to the helicopter.

Vanderbilt had thought of danger and looked up.
Grant, more cunning or perhaps only more needy,
saw another weapon. He was not sure what would
happen when he tried to use it, only what would
happen if he did not. It would be difficult: the projection of a stabilizer from the tapering fuselage made

the angle critical. But he would contrive a way of using it—if not on the pilot, then on himself. One way or another, unless Vanderbilt got psychic and turned back now, one of them was going to take a dive into the tail rotor.

He backed away: away from the open door, but more importantly towards the rear of the machine. "I'm not getting in that plane." He let his voice run up thin and ready, as if with fear. It required almost no acting at all. Stumbling backwards he waited until he was behind the guarding fin, then deliberately turned one ankle under him. The ground came up to hit him again and he accepted the blow with resignation.

The pilot moved towards him automatically. "Get up, for Christ's sake." Grant rolled clumsily onto his face, leaving Vanderbilt's heavy coat behind, and got his knees under him. He hauled his body upright with muscles he did not know he had, and then he waited.

Vanderbilt may have been a little psychic, for he turned then and looked back down the hill. He saw Grant kneeling, head bowed, in the grass and Piet moving towards him. It was a big field, from halfway up the hill the figures looked like dolls; even the big machine looked like a toy. For a moment, frowning, he studied what they were doing, down where the shadows were gathering.

Before he was aware of having solved the puzzle he was running, driving down the hill as fast as his strong legs could push his big body, mouth agape with a shout the slipstream threw back in his throat, a warning that had no chance of reaching its mark and which would anyway have been too late.

When the pilot was between him and the rotor Grant launched himself from his crouch like a hun-

dred-metre runner from his blocks. The crown of his
head pitched into the pit of Piet's stomach with a
force that drove all the wind out of him in a surprised
grunt. He staggered back, folding, but Grant kept
coming, hands tied back and head low, still pushing
hard, so that their two bodies described an attenuated parabola, a seemingly endless fall.

Vanderbilt, watching spellbound even as he ran,
could not believe that reality could be so long sus-
pended as to allow it. The pilot had to fall, or Grant to
weaken, or one of them to realize the enormity of
what was happening. It was too improbable, too bi-
zarre: like watching a crazy old man weaving magic
with a couple of sticks only to have the magic confirmed by a shovelful of wet sand.

The long fall and Vanderbilt's certainty that the
laws of physics would intervene in time ended together with a shrill clatter and a thump.

Grant lay face down in the grass, still except for the
heaving of his shoulders over his labouring lungs.

The damaged rotor had gone on turning until the
bent ends had hacked enough from their tips and
from the skin of the tail that they could turn freely
and without screaming once more.

The pilot died where he had fallen, cartwheeled by
the spinning blade; not then but soon, before Vanderbilt had to consider his obligations to a man whose
life might possibly be saved.

After he was dead Vanderbilt, feeling ten years
older and twenty pounds heavier, rose stiffly from
where he had been kneeling at his friend's head,
helpless to comfort in the face of appalling injury,
and walked towards Grant. Grant had rolled onto his
side in order to watch. Vanderbilt walked slowly, giving himself time to refine a response. He felt an urgent, almost rapine desire to lay into Grant—bound

and downed as he was—with his boots and his fists and anything he could lay his hands on, and reduce him to a bloody pulp. But Pretoria wanted him unharmed. He had thought that odd at the time: in the light of subsequent events it seemed insane. Pretoria's demands—together, Vanderbilt was willing to admit, for he was no more blind to his faults than to those of other people, with his own mistakes—had cost a good and useful man his life.

Towering silently over the man on the ground, quaking gently with quiet rage, Vanderbilt watched the fear in Grant's eyes. Apart from the time he had been unconscious, it had been there all the fourteen hours they had known each other. It was still there, but changed—hysterical terror transmuted into a wholly rational fear of likely and imminent assault. Beside that there was a kind of grim satisfaction. He was breathing fast but mostly with exertion.

Vanderbilt said woodenly, "You aren't going to tell me that was an accident."

"Damn sure it was no accident."

"Then *why?*"

"You're kidding. That bastard was going to get me killed. I got him first."

"What are you talking about?" demanded Vanderbilt. "He was a *pilot. I* can get you killed; he could only get you delivered."

"You can only get me killed here. He'd have got me killed in Pretoria. That's two separate propositions. I told you—I'm not going back."

Vanderbilt passed a hand across his face. It shook very slightly, but neither Grant nor anyone else would have mistaken the tremor for weakness. "Sonny, I could get very tired of hearing what you are and are not going to do."

"Then cut me loose and I won't bother you again."

Vanderbilt regarded him thoughtfully for a moment. Then he said, "Can you get up?"

"Yes." He had managed when it mattered. Grant began the clumsy caterpillar manoeuvre that would bring him to his feet.

Vanderbilt let him get halfway before launching a vicious, measured kick that took him in the side of the knee. Grant's head snapped back and pain whistled through his teeth. He crashed on his side on the ground, rolling, lacking the hands to comfort himself.

Vanderbilt nodded slowly. "That should keep you in one place for a while." He turned his back on Grant and bent over the sprawled body of the pilot, and began the horrid task of stripping it.

2

Nathan Shola spent most of the night on the phone. At first he was calling his people, members of his army in exile, semi-retired warriors, some of whom were bus-drivers and some of whom were surgeons, and then they were calling him back with what they had been able to discover. By dawn he had compiled a list of people in the UK—South Africans, South African sympathizers, people with business interests in the country—to whom Vanderbilt could turn for assistance. It was not a fully comprehensive list, but it did include all the most likely names, especially those with access to air transport. The bus-men called in sick and the surgeons rescheduled their operations, and by breakfast time each of the people on the list was under surveillance.

Except a company pilot named Jan-Pieter van Dam, who was already being sought by his employers on the grounds that not only was he inexplicably absent but so was his machine.

Shola was about to telephone chief Inspector Corner with a description of the helicopter when Chief Inspector Corner rang him to say a police car was on its way round to him. Something had turned up on which he would like Mr. Shola's opinion.

"Not Joel?"

"Not as far as we can make out," the policeman replied ominously.

The car climbed quickly onto the backbone of England, moorland filling in behind it like a rising tide. The driver knew no more than that he had been given directions he had grave doubts about being able to follow.

Shola presumed they had arrived when the car left the rutted road to drive across two fields, and in the third were several vehicles and a helicopter. A number of men were scattered about the field; Shola recognized the chief inspector in a small knot clustered around a tartan rug on the grass close by the helicopter. The car stopped nearby and he walked over to join them.

The thing under the rug was evidently a body. Shola tried to estimate its proportions. He decided it was too short to be Grant, but that could have been how it was lying. Or, if he had interpreted Chief Inspector Corner's remark correctly, how much of it was left.

When they peeled the rug stickily back he knew it was not Grant, although he could not have said why he was so sure. It was not the face: there was not enough of it to judge.

The chief inspector indicated the battered rotor. "He seems to have walked into that."

"Did he walk, or was he pushed?"

"Ah. Well, if he isn't Grant he's probably the pilot, and if he's the pilot he almost certainly didn't walk."

Shola said, with conviction and surprise and quite a lot of pride, "Then Joel did this."

Corner had also reached that conclusion. "What makes you think so?"

"Joel didn't bring that helicopter here, the Boer did. Vanderbilt. It was his ride out. By the same token, Joel needs desperately to stay in this country. Killing the pilot and bending the machine bought him time. As long as it takes Vanderbilt to set up another meet, that's how long we have to find him. This"—he indicated the mess on the grass—"won't happen again. If Joel is fighting, he'll get no more chances. By now he'll be trussed up hand and foot, blindfolded, gagged and probably with a couple of ribs stove in for good measure."

"But not dead?"

"There's only one body here, Mr. Corner. If Vanderbilt had killed Joel it would have been here, while he was angry; and he wouldn't have gone to the trouble of stripping a corpse for his benefit."

Chief Inspector Corner gave him a wan smile. "You aren't exactly new to the business of deduction, are you, Mr. Shola?"

The black man smiled back. "Terrorism is a hard school. An ability to draw inferences accurately is essential. Without it one would be wiser to stick to clerking."

They moved away from the tartan rug. Two men with a stretcher took their places. The policeman said, "Is that what you did, before?"

"Before I became a terrorist, you mean?"

Corner permitted himself a weary sigh. "Mr. Shola, if you think I am unaware of your background, and that of Joel Grant, your logic is serving you less well than you believe. I think we might make better progress if you stop trying to shock me."

Shola accepted the rebuke gracefully. "I was a legal clerk in Port Elizabeth. One day my principal asked why I was depressed: wasn't the money good enough or what? The money was pretty good, for a black clerk, but we weren't winning many cases— not the cases I was interested in. He agreed. But he couldn't think what more he could do: the system was loaded against what he and I, and you, would call justice for blacks. He had already tried everything short of blowing things up. If I had any suggestions he would be interested to hear them. I gave a lot of thought to what he had said. Then I gave him my resignation and started blowing things up." He watched the policeman with a quizzical half-smile.

Corner said gently, "If you're waiting for a round of applause we could be here some time."

Shola laughed aloud, drawing curious glances. "Don't worry, Chief Inspector, I know better than to expect you to condone armed struggle. But things are different in my country. Here my friend is abducted in violent and mysterious circumstances and the police search for him. In South Africa it would be the police who had him."

Corner sniffed. "I'm so glad you're happy with our work," he said dryly. "If you were happy enough to leave it to us I'd be ecstatic."

Shola feigned incomprehension. "I'm sorry?"

Corner breathed heavily. "For the last four hours, every line of enquiry my men have tried to follow up they have had an audience. Dusky gentlemen of non-indigenous antecedents have watched them go in and watched them come out. Once or twice could be a coincidence, but it's getting ridiculous."

Shola grinned. "We're only trying to be helpful."

"I dare say," said Corner. "But another of our national characteristics, besides not liking our policemen abducting political embarrassments, is this general aversion to private armies."

"A double handful of ex-patriot Africans hardly amounts to a private army. We're just trying to give you an edge. We all have experience of these people, and for Joel's sake we want you to have the benefit of it. For instance, I may be able to tell you two things you don't yet know about the man under that rug. One is his name."

"I know his name," Corner growled.

"I knew his name before I knew you'd found him. The other thing is that that helicopter is a short-range job—four hundred odd miles. Nobody would set off across two continents in it. Nor does the company which owns it and employed the pilot have a long-haul aircraft."

It was true that Chief Inspector Corner had not yet received that information. No doubt somebody was getting it together for him now, but he was too good a policeman to stick to channels when a short cut could get him to the same place quicker. He latched onto Shola's train of thought without missing a beat. "So our macerated friend wasn't flying them out of the country, or at least not this trip. He was taking them to a rendezvous—with a bigger plane, or maybe a ship. My God, we'd have to freeze up every airfield and harbour in the land to be sure of stopping them."

"Theoretically. But it would be logical"—Shola smiled very faintly—"to start with airports close to London and the south coast ports. Anywhere north of Birmingham and Vanderbilt would have driven there: it wouldn't have been worth his while waiting for the helicopter. Also, until he found Suzanne he didn't even know where I was, let alone where Joel was; but his escape route would have been set up before he left Pretoria. They would work on the statistical probability of finding us in the largest centre of population: whatever plans they laid were based on London. But they knew they could be unlucky, so the helicopter was laid on in case it was needed. Look south, Mr. Corner."

"Heathrow," mused Corner. "Gatwick, Stanstead. Tilbury, Southampton, Dover—Bristol? Oh yes, that narrows it down nicely."

Liz ached to sleep off the jetlag but could not afford the time. She showered at her hotel, changed into a dress that shouted London and a picture hat, and carefully (for she did not practise all that often) applied make-up. She wanted people to spot her for an English tourist, and to take her for the kind of visitor they could tell a thing or two about this land.

Pretoria was not London; it was not even Manchester. The number of places where a woman could go in search of plausibly casual conversation with Afrikaner men was limited. She asked the desk clerk to direct her to the city's art galleries, museums, exhibitions of any sort. She spent the afternoon in a cultural daze, smiling a lot and chatting to everyone she could. Twelve times she was welcomed to South Africa, two or three times she received distinctly funny looks and once she was propositioned.

Finally, in an art gallery, she realized that the young man discoursing so knowledgeably on Rubens was a member of the security police. He was using his day off as he apparently used most of them, indulging a passion for European Old Masters. Liz was not naive enough to find that paradoxical, but she was a little surprised to find herself liking him.

He persuaded her to have a drink with him, in much the same way that an impala persuades a cheetah, and she persuaded him to take just a little more wine than he was used to. By late afternoon, when they parted with an almost archaic politeness and a firm date for the museum on his next day off, Liz knew—almost without probing, certainly he would never know he had been grilled—that De Witte was still in hospital awaiting major heart surgery; that despite this and despite his desk being occupied by a man who had every right to call and consider himself acting chief, De Witte himself still ran his department as far as anything important was concerned; and that something very important and top echelon was going on which had upset the most inquisitive members of that highly inquisitive establishment by proving utterly impervious to even professional snooping.

Liz did not know if the repatriation of a former terrorist could possibly be a part of such high-level intrigue, but she left the art-lover knowing where she had to go to pursue her enquiries. She had to take them to De Witte.

That which was fancifully described as his luncheon consumed, Joachim De Witte settled reluctantly into the long grey afternoon that yawned, a vacancy, before him. Afternoon was when he was supposed to rest. Strictly speaking he was supposed to rest all the time, but the hospital had had to make concessions to his commitments. That morning he had seen Botha for an hour—to bring him up to date on the activities of the department he was ostensibly running: poor Walter Botha had been considerably put out on his first visit to find its purpose the precise opposite of what he had supposed—and his secretary for ninety minutes, and this evening Elinor would be here, talking and knitting and generally replenishing his flask of human contentment.

He knew of no way in which she was a remarkable woman, but missing her was an ache: when he woke alone in the night, when she was not there come dawn; not so much during his busy morning but all through the grey tunnel of the afternoon until they brought what was fancifully described as his tea and he could start listening for her footsteps.

The distinctive tap of a woman's shoes, but not nurses' shoes, drew his attention now. The tattoo stopped outside his door. Presently he heard voices, low at first, then louder. Then the woman said, very clearly, "I have never heard anything so witless in my life."

De Witte could contain his curiosity no longer. He filled his lungs and bellowed, "What the hell is going on out there?"

One of the men watching his door opened it a few inches to show an apologetic, well-scrubbed face. "Sorry, sir. It's a young lady—"

"It's nothing of the sort," Liz said briskly, elbowing past him. "It's Elizabeth—Hettie's daughter from England." She stopped at the foot of the bed, smiling at him; gradually the smile faded and the eyes became puzzled. "Uncle Paul?"

De Witte had never been called Paul, did not have a sister by Hettie or any other name, and knew of no relatives in England. But the long afternoons were very boring, and he was considerably in the mood for illicit conversation with a tall, green-eyed girl he had never seen before. His circle of acquaintance had narrowed claustrophobically in hospital. He had taken to thinking of it as Robben Island with enemas.

He waved a calming hand at the worried guard and said solemnly, "And how is your mother?"

The girl smiled again, though still a shade uncertainly. "She's fine—up to her blue rinse in other people's business, you know mother, this month it's the turn of the Comforts Fund for Parish Pensioners, even the scarecrow in the turnip field has lost his muffler, and who she imagines is going to benefit from my last year's swimsuit I hate to think."

De Witte grinned, enjoying himself. "Sit down, girl, make yourself at home. I reckon Hettie hasn't changed too much, then. It's a long time, mind, must be—"

"*Ages,*" Liz supplied emphatically. "You know, I hardly recognized you, but then I could only have been—"

"Oh—like so, only," said De Witte, waving a hand vaguely over the bedspread at an indeterminate infant height.

"Well, maybe a bit more," said Liz, and they both laughed.

It was clear to Liz that De Witte was playing a game; probably quite an innocuous one, certainly he had no reason to suspect her of anything more sinister than mistaking the identity of a long-lost relative. She presumed he was teasing her for his own amusement. She could live with that: his sport served her ends well enough. She had managed to meet him, was already laying the foundations for a kind of friendship, and would soon divert the discourse along more profitable routes. First it was necessary to protect herself.

"You gave me the devil of a turn," she said, "when I finally found your address only to have your housekeeper say you'd been taken to hospital bleeding like a stuck pig. For heaven's sake, Uncle Paul, how long

have you been using a chainsaw?—and you still can't
do it right. I didn't know whether I'd find you in
stitches in casualty or in pieces in the morgue. And
then when I asked for you at the desk it was as if I'd
discovered the secret hideaway of Joseph Mengele.
Whatever have you been doing to deserve all"—she
helplessly indicated the door, now closed—"this?"

"I'm an important man," De Witte said modestly.
His voice was deep and musical, rich with subtle
modulation.

"An important carpenter? Well, all right," agreed
Liz, "I suppose you wouldn't be the first, but what
are they guarding you against? How many enemies
does a cabinet-maker make?"

Not without some regret, De Witte decided it was
time to come clean. He ran up the flagpole his most
charming smile. "I'm afraid, my dear Elizabeth,
you've been misled. I'm not a carpenter."

Liz feigned surprise. "You're not? But mother
said—"

"Nor," he continued solemnly, "am I related to nor
so far as I know acquainted with your mother. I am
an impostor. My name is Joachim De Witte and I
work for the government. I'm sorry, I have been
enjoying your company under false pretences."

He met her gaze, ready for anger, embarrassment,
rebuke. He was not prepared for, though delighted
by, the laughter that welled from her, deep in her
throat and brilliant in her eyes. Her eyes were as
green as only a cat's had any right to be.

"You mean I've got the wrong De Witte?" She
chuckled. "Oh, for pity's sake. And you!—you might
have told me. But listen, you must be related, you
two—how many De Wittes are there in this town?"

"A few," he allowed with a smile. "As far as I know
I have no woodworking relative called Paul."

Liz was still grinning. "Well I have, and thanks to your rather juvenile sense of humour he's been suffering in neglect while I've been exchanging family gossip with a total stranger. I have to find out what's happened to him."

"Of course; I'm sorry." He was more sorry to see her going. "Do you want to use the phone?"

She thought quickly. "Yes, thanks—it might save me another wasted journey." Her boy's grin took the sting out of the comment. "How do I get reception?" He gave her the number and she carefully dialled another, screening the dial casually with her handbag.

She got the laundry. She spoke quickly, making the most of a pause while the supervisor went to close a door between herself and her machines in the obvious hope that this might help her make sense of the conversation.

Liz said, "I was with you a few minutes ago, looking for a De Witte. Well, I've found one but he isn't mine. This one's clearly in for psychiatric treatment whereas mine has a cut foot." She smiled disarmingly at the subject of her insult. "She's checking."

The woman in the laundry said, rather kindly, "Look, I don't know—maybe you have the wrong extension?"

"Hello, yes," said Liz inexplicably. "He is? Oh, that's good. We must have passed on the road. I'll call the house then. I'm sorry to have given you so much trouble."

"Er—no trouble," said the laundry supervisor, replacing her receiver with the care she customarily reserved for items fresh from the autoclave.

"Well," said Liz, "the riddle of the missing uncle appears to be solved. He was never admitted: they fired a couple of stitches into him and sent him home. Have you a phonebook?"

"Underneath."

"You don't mind?"

"The least I can do."

She chose a number at random. A man answered in Afrikaans. He did not sound happy to be disturbed. "Uncle Paul? At last! It's Liz—I'm at the hospital, I've been trailing you half-way round this damn town. Are you all right?"

The man at the other end said irritably, "What? Who is that? Ruthie, is this one of your jokes?"

"Thank God," said Liz with feeling. "I thought I'd arrived just in time for your funeral. Stay put, I'll be right round."

"Ruthie? I'm telling you, I've had enough of your funny sense of humour."

"Oh," said Liz, taken aback. "Oh, well in that case I suppose you'd better go straight to bed. Never mind, I'll come round in the morning, we can talk then."

"Ruthie, you're going to make me angry. I mean it—"

"Sleep tight, I'll see you tomorrow." She put down the phone. "The painkillers they gave him are putting him to sleep. I'll go see him in the morning."

"His foot's all right then?" De Witte enquired politely.

"Just sore enough to make him more careful in future." She picked up her bag and started to leave. "Well, thank you for the use of the phone—and the conversation, it was most interesting."

De Witte let her get to the door. She tasted failure. Then he said, "Do you have to go?"

3

Vanderbilt allowed himself the luxury of sleep. He slept with his clothes on, with his shoes on, with one ear tuned for trouble. He first took pains to secure his prisoner against the triple temptations of escape, assault and self-destruction, and then he slept: for six glorious, uninterrupted hours. It was enough, if need be, to see him through the next two days, and if by then he was not in the pipeline back to Pretoria it would be time to start thinking of cutting himself loose from his burden and making his way home alone. But no dark thoughts of defeat came to disturb his rest. He slept without dreaming.

He woke before dawn, as he had intended to, without haste or alarm but immediately and wholly and without wondering where he was. He knew where he was: curled, not altogether comfortably, across the front seats of the big maroon car with the steering wheel pressing into his thigh and his feet hanging out of the open door. His left arm, pillowed double under his head, had gone numb.

Stretching carefully in the absolute dark, he sat up. He scratched his head and shook life back into his arm. Then he felt for the door light and screwed the bulb back. The pale luminosity that sprang up seemed briefly to fill the barn until his eyes, adjusting, put its power into perspective.

He had found the barn in the same way he had found the stone house the night before. It was almost empty: only a few rows of mouldering hay and the musky scent of departed cattle remained to tell its function. Towards the end of summer the hay would be replenished, ready for the cattle to return with

the winter, but until then the barn had no role except
as a refuge. Owls used it, and martins, and Vanderbilt
had driven the car inside and closed the big wooden
doors as confident of privacy as they. There was no
other building in sight. Vanderbilt and the martins
slept while the owls hunted.

Grant got no sleep, which was also as Vanderbilt
had intended. Crucified against the front bumper he
could neither sit up nor lie down; the muscles of his
shoulders and arms, unnaturally stretched along the
chrome tree, bore half his weight and six hours of it
reduced his body to a rigid, throbbing crucible of
agony that he could not ease. Any attempt at movement brought the tears pricking to his eyes in the
dark.

Vanderbilt, strolling round the bonnet with torch
in hand, greeted him amiably. Grant replied with the
grossest Afrikaans obscenity he could think of. Vanderbilt smiled. He noted with satisfaction the tracks
of tears through the dirt on Grant's thin cheeks, the
red-raw bracelets of skin where his wrists were roped
to the car, the knotted muscles of his shoulders inside
the bloody borrowed shirt, and the way his belly
heaved to draw enough air into his lungs to swear by.
The big man catalogued the hurts with professional
detachment. Then he indulged in a lazy grin. "You
want to try for the hundred yards' dash again, boy?"

Grant's eyes burned with red-rimmed hatred.
"Against you, fat man? Any time. You're slow—even
downhill you're slow."

The grin died on Vanderbilt's lips. He said quietly,
"You'll be wiser not reminding me of that."

"Why, what'll you do—kill me?"

Vanderbilt backed away thoughtfully. He shared
with other bulky men an almost balletic grace of
movement. "Of course not." He sauntered to the car

door, reached inside for his coat, and then slammed it very hard. In the confined space and the quiet it sounded like a gunshot.

The explosive tremor ran through Grant's racked body like nails, forcing from him a thin cry. Pain, rage and humiliation warred in him. Light chiselled at his clenched eyes: through the distorting film of saline he saw the Boer squatting before him.

"But I can do a lot to you short of killing you," Vanderbilt confided seriously. "And just because I can see that, from your point of view, the murder of my friend was something of a necessity, you mustn't get the idea that I forgive you."

He produced a knife and laid the blade of it chill on Grant's cheek, the diamond tip just puckering the outer canthus of his eye. Grant breathed shallowly through his mouth. After a moment Vanderbilt took the knife away and cut the rope from his wrists.

There was nothing to eat, but a tap beside the door delivered rusty water from a raintap. Vanderbilt drank and washed, then let Grant drink, awkwardly one-handed, the other coupled by the handcuffs to a convenient manger. By the light of the torch resting on the car roof Vanderbilt watched him: speculatively, aware that when he worked off the kinks of his wretched night it would be necessary to handicap him in some other way, but also curiously. Joel Grant was as much an enigma to him now as when he first leafed through his file in Botha's office: a white man who not only ran with black terrorists but was sufficiently valued by them that they risked, and ultimately lost, their entire organization on his account.

Why? Friendship, possibly—he might once, in another time and place, have been capable of commanding that kind of loyalty, before De Witte took him apart and well-meaning experts cobbled him together with sentimentality like well-chewed string when the decent thing would have been to put him out of his misery. Vanderbilt had seen enough interrogations, and the human consequences of them, to hope that if his turn ever came someone would be sufficiently careless to let him die. Grant clearly felt the same, but Vanderbilt had not done this job so well so long without learning how to separate duty from inclination and which to put first.

Or if not friendship, perhaps because he had represented some kind of symbol to them. The political potential of a white South African supporting Mpani, not only with noble sentiments but with body and finally soul, would have been considerable, but only while Mpani lived and his group survived. A crippled ex-member of a defunct organization living in obscure and sour exile half-way across the world could be of little worth to the black African cause and consequently of no interest to white Africa. So why was Pretoria so determined to recover him? No information he had clung to could be of any relevance now.

So why was Joel Grant important enough to risk an international incident in a country whose support was craved by South Africa?—not to mention the loss (Vanderbilt entertained no false modesty about his own usefulness) of a valuable agent. And why had Botha not explained, at least in broad terms? It was true that the task could be performed in ignorance, and that needless secrecy might be no more than the vanity of a rather small man placed unexpectedly in a rather large job. But Vanderbilt was uneasy. He was accustomed to the machinations of those who opposed him in the countries where he operated: he did not expect to find himself working in the dark against a backdrop of intrigue at home.

More than half to himself, and therefore surprised

when he received an answer, Vanderbilt murmured, "What do they want you for really?"

Grant looked up, animal furtive, from his drinking and peered at the bulky shadow which was all he could pick out by the backwash of the torch. "You mean you don't know?"

Vanderbilt shrugged. "I don't need to know. It makes no difference. I'm curious, is all, as to what could possibly make you worth all this trouble."

Grant was at a loss to know how to reply. Incredibly, his pride was involved: he could not bring himself to accede to Vanderbilt's overt opinion that he was a military and political has-been. He fabricated a sardonic sneer with which to turn back to the tap. "Unfinished business."

Vanderbilt nodded understanding. "So you don't know either."

Grant glowered at him. By degrees, however, the anger turned to a kind of bitter humour in his torchlit face. "Hey, you think maybe you've got the wrong man?"

Vanderbilt grinned back. "Like maybe it's actually your twin brother we should be after?"

"The one I don't know about, since we were separated at birth."

"I believe that's traditional," agreed Vanderbilt.

"So is everyone living happily ever after."

"Maybe De Witte will turn out to be your fairy godmother."

Grant winced. "For five months after I got out of Pretoria I couldn't hear his name without throwing up. Wherever I was, however inconvenient. I once did a comprehensive redecoration of some woman at a party. She only wanted to talk about the weather, but the Swedish accent had me fooled."

Vanderbilt laughed out loud. "You know Gilbert

and Sullivan? You know the one about the boy who's supposed to be a pilot, only his nurse mishears and gets him apprenticed to a pirate? You ever wonder if maybe something similar happened to you?"

Again, Grant's pride was touched. His jaw came up. "I took you, at the house, and your friend with the helicopter, with both hands tied behind my back. If I'm inept, what does that make you?" He straightened as much as the short chain and his own cramped muscles would permit, waiting to be hit.

Vanderbilt's grin died away entirely but he made no move towards the tied man. His voice was quiet and level. "It makes me careless, both times. I underestimated you. I'm doing it again. The reminder is timely. But Piet did his job well enough. I told you, he wasn't like me, he was—"

"I know: a pilot. So how good was his nurse's hearing?"

After a longish pause Vanderbilt said softly, "You really are a little shit, aren't you?"

"Not at all," said Joel Grant, "I'm five foot eight and a half."

The boot of the car, though capacious, measured only four feet and change. Having already spent some time in it Grant was reluctant to submit to the experience again, but a judicious fist to the belly doubled him over and then he fitted easily. With his hands behind him once more, his feet lashed to the spare wheel and the handkerchief gag—Vanderbilt at least had the grace to rinse it through under the tap first—back in his mouth, he was as incapable of communicating his situation as a sardine in a can. Vanderbilt could with absolute confidence have parked on a police forecourt.

"I have a phone call to make," he said. "After that, hopefully, we'll have some idea what we're doing.

Don't you worry about a thing—I'll get you home, see if I don't." He closed the boot, shutting Grant—again like a sardine—into a tin tomb smelling of oil.

Vanderbilt found a telephone kiosk and a pillar-box at a crossroads midway between two minuscule hamlets neither of which was big enough to command a sub-post office. He dialled from memory and the call was answered on the first ring. Vanderbilt and his controller exchanged identification codes and moved immediately into Afrikaans.

"Where the hell are you?"

"North Yorkshire moors, so far as I can make out."

"You've still got Grant?"

"Oh yes. But Piet's dead."

"Christ! How?"

Vanderbilt explained tersely, then asked, "Have they found the helicopter yet?"

"If they have they're keeping it under their hats."

"So maybe they haven't. Anyway, I'm well clear of the area now. Listen, I'm going to keep travelling north. Scrub Gatwick: have a plane meet me at Glasgow."

"Glasgow? For Christ's sake, Danny, what do we know about Glasgow? We always use the southern airports, we have friends there, we know our way around."

"Exactly. And we're known, and useful as that may have been in the past, this time it could get me nailed. This isn't the usual thing: in, hit and out before anybody's sure what's happened. This time we've been unlucky—or careless, or something. They know something is happening, they probably have a fair idea what and they damn sure know who. They know where we operate: they'll be watching Gatwick like hawks, and the rest of the south for good measure.

"But Glasgow? They think like you, nobody chooses to go north of Birmingham and nobody even considers going north of Carlisle. Special Branch thinks the world ends abruptly on the banks of the Trent. Well, I'm not embarking on a seven-hour drive into a noose that will draw tighter with every mile. The plane at Gatwick—leave it there, it'll give them something to watch. But find me another and have it meet me at Glasgow. I'm maybe five, six hours away: we can be out of the country by tonight if you can fix the plane. I'll check back with you later."

The controller remained deeply uneasy. For one thing he was more used to delivering instructions than taking them. "Danny, I don't think Botha's going to like—"

"Sod Botha. When I get home I shall take a lot of convincing that Botha actually knew what he was doing with this. De Witte will back me. Now for pity's sake stop arguing and get that aeroplane organized. And do it properly: I don't want to pull off my end of it only to have us boarded because somebody tried to shortcut the paperwork."

He banged the receiver down, then paused for a moment in the shabby kiosk, listening to the echo of his anger. He did not know the reason for it. No one had let him down; he had been, as he had said, unlucky or careless, but nobody was to blame, probably not even himself. He was not particularly deep in the mire; at any event, he had successfully extricated himself from deeper. But he could not rid himself of the feeling that the enterprise was in some obscure way ill-starred. He returned to the car and let in the clutch with a bad-tempered bang lest his passenger should escape the effects of his mood. He drove north-west.

Chief Inspector Corner's gentle reprimand notwith-
standing, the dusky gentlemen of non-indigenous
antecedents—to whom Shola had once unforgivably
and unforgettably referred as the Kaffia—continued
to use whatever position, influence and talents they
could command to pry wherever experience told
them they would be least warmly welcomed. In the
course of a few hours they compiled a short-list of
aircraft which would have surprised no one by suddenly taking off for South Africa, and of those one
was generally seen as odds-on favourite.

The Britannia had been on the ground at Gatwick
for two days, although its cargo of lead crystal, china
dinner services and agricultural spares had been
loaded and ready to leave within hours of its arrival.
It was owned by an Anglo-French concern and its
declared destination was North-West Africa. Casual
enquiries about the delay met with the reply that
there was some doubt about the consignee's credit-
worthiness and that a guarantor was being sought.
The pilot was an Englishman: however, research re-
vealed family connections with the old Rhodesia. It
was all highly speculative: it was the best they could
come up with. Shola contacted Chief Inspector Corner: Corner made pointed remarks and then arranged for a discreet watch to be kept on the suspect
aeroplane.

But Shola had his doubts. "If she's been there for
two days she was laid on before the business with the
helicopter."

Corner agreed. "The helicopter was to take them
down there. It would have been quicker than driving, safer than driving and would have made it easier
to transfer Grant onto the plane without being noticed."

"All right. But they lost the helicopter, in circumstances which were bound to attract attention before long. So what does Vanderbilt do next? Embark on that long dangerous drive that's more dangerous now than when he first rejected it? He's no fool: he'll know that we've connected him with this, he may be working on the assumption that we're closer to him than we are. He can't call up another helicopter without the risk that it'll bring us to him. So he's stuck with the car. Even if he changes it, he knows we have a description of him, probably a name and photograph to go with it by now. He has about as much chance of getting into Gatwick undetected as I have of attending a National Front meeting."

Again the chief inspector agreed. "But how many options has he? He doesn't want to settle down here with Grant and raise a family—he wants to go home. That probably means an aircraft, conceivably a ship. Yes, it's dangerous, but sometime, somewhere he has to risk it."

"Not until he's worked out an edge. Having us stake out a Britannia at Gatwick while he saunters aboard a DC3 at Aberdeen might appeal to his sense of humour as well as saving his skin."

"They have one? A sense of humour?" Corner sounded surprised.

"Not as much as they used to have," admitted Shola. "They used to think that the idea of majority rule in South Africa was funny."

"Very well," said Corner briskly. "So having advised me to look south, having let me set up expensive cordons around large areas of the southern counties, having in fact helped me to identify an individual aeroplane as the likely instrument of escape, you now tell me you've changed your mind and Aberdeen is nice at this time of year."

Shola grinned. "Dead unreliable, us Kaffirs. No, I

haven't changed my mind. I think that was his plan. I'll go further: I think it very likely the Britannia was his plane, and that it's still waiting for him. But I think that, about now or maybe a bit earlier, he'll be changing his mind. He and I are in the same line of business, remember. If it was me, I'd be worried about the amount of time that's passing. About now I'd be thinking that the risks of setting up a new escape route would be less than those of sticking to an original which has already gone badly wrong and which has been kicking around long enough for someone who shouldn't have got wind of it. Aberdeen," he added graciously, "was only a for instance. Anywhere that wasn't south would do.

"And I'd be particularly interested if any of the planes you're watching should take off unexpectedly this morning for any of the northern airports, with or without a cargo. Not the Britannia, though; he'll want us to keep watching that."

"This Vanderbilt: do you know him?" Corner's shrewd eyes were on him. "You sound as if you know him."

"Oh yes," said Shola softly, "I know him. Not personally, you understand; not even by repute, although I've heard the name. But I know him. He's me: a man fighting for the future of his country as he wants it to be. He's tough and he's clever and he's brave, and he knows that when you're far from home and surrounded by enemies, sometimes all the toughness and cleverness and courage in the world aren't enough to stand between you and twenty years behind high walls, when the only freedom you'll enjoy will be going bald. And he'll risk that three or four times every year, until he's caught or killed or his nerve goes."

"You sound as if you admire him."

"I hate the bastard."

4

Liz paused at the door and swung him a look compounded in equal parts of humour and severity. "Why, are there some more of my relatives you'd like to impersonate?"

De Witte chuckled deeply, sending a tremor through the frame of his bed. "No, you've seen my entire repertoire, I'm afraid. I'm sorry, girl. I plead total crashing boredom as mitigation."

Liz threw a glance round the small white room. "Have you been here long?"

"Subjectively or objectively? Objectively, several weeks. Subjectively, half my bloody life."

Liz waited a moment longer. Then, with a smile, she dropped her bag on the table, threw her hat on top of it and dropped into the chair. "Okay. Hell, I've nothing better to do. Till Uncle Paul wakes up I don't know a soul in this whole country." She looked frankly at the machines ranged at his bedhead, the tubes and leads hung round him. "What are you in for?—If it's something embarrassing, feel free to lie."

"It was embarrassing, all right," De Witte said grimly. He was thinking of the ease with which he had been taken by a little black scrap who could have been one of his wife's housegirls. "But not biologically so. I was mugged. They rushed me in here and did a lovely repair job, but if I'd have known what was coming I'd have stuck a plaster on and gone home, because once they had me at their mercy the doctors started finding all sorts of things wrong with me. I only came in with a little nick in my chest. Now

I've got a defective heart, my insurance agent is sending me grapes and my accountant is regretting the life membership he talked me into buying at the country club."

Liz sucked in a deep, quiet breath. She was under no illusions about what she was hearing. The man was dying and he knew it and cared very much, and still from somewhere he could dredge up the courage to joke about it with a perfect stranger. With the same instinctive generosity with which she devoted time and energy to the defeat of Joel Grant's daemons—ingenuously, without calculation, for no better reason than a purely personal willingness to answer a perceived need—she leaned forward and laid her hand in an unmistakable gesture of comfort on the bare forearm, above the taped drip-tube, of the man whom—intellectually, philosophically—she abhorred more than any other.

She hated everything he stood for, the most fundamental precepts on which he had built his life and his work. She hated what he had done to people she cared about and to others of whom she knew nothing. She hated his long fingers creeping spiderlike across the world and their prurient rape of her precious privacy. But she found she could not hate the man: this strong man, lying like a felled lion under a maypole from a machine, all his restless ranging and seeking and striving condensed at this ignoble last into a small room like a cage.

The tragedy of his reduction, from sun king to shadow man, touched her: not with compassion exactly, inside where it finally counted he was still too strong to need or want kindly consolations, but with a sorrow that recognized the vacuum that would remain when Joachim De Witte was gone. She said quietly, "So what happens now?"

The white moustache flared briefly in a wry facial shrug. "They make tests. They take blood samples. I ask, 'Will the tests cure me? Will taking my blood away make my heart beat stronger?' They smile at me as if I am a child and shake their stupid fingers in my face. There are a lot of things they can do, they say, and the tests will help them decide what is best. But actually they do nothing, and as the days go by I feel my life growing thin, dilute, and seeping away through the cracks. And I think there is nothing they can do."

A dove-grey silence settled in the room like ash. De Witte broke it after a minute with an unexpected chuckle. "Elinor—my wife, Elinor—thinks they will give me a new heart."

Liz looked up startled. "Really?" Momentarily her senses reeled in the vortex of logic which is the South African paradox: that this land where television is a suspiciously radical innovation was the birthplace and nursery of heart transplant surgery. She fumbled to recover her grip on the conversation. "Well—perhaps they will."

Although De Witte's sick heart seemed far removed from the purpose which had brought her six thousand miles, for the moment any conversation she could have with him was sufficient. As long as he was talking to her, as long as she had access to him, she held the initiative. Sooner or later, in small pieces, unknowing, or all at once in angry response to a direct question, he would tell her about Grant. The urgency of her quest made her long to force the pace, to quiz him and risk the consequences, but prudence won over impatience. Finesse was the key to his knowledge. She needed to charm the snake, not bludgeon him.

De Witte shook his leonine head. "No chance. Not for me. My heart's one off."

"On moral grounds? Or are you just boasting?"

He grinned at her. It was a pleasant change for him, being able to talk about it without the heavy undertones. "You're pretty hard to impress, cousin Liz. No, I'm a practical man, I can claim to be unique on strictly demonstrable evidence. I got funny blood."

"Funny blood?"

"And funny tissue to go with it. Well, call it rare—it isn't all that much of a laughing matter when successful transplants depend on a good match between donor and recipient. The chances of somebody else with funny blood dying considerately enough as to leave his funny heart available for transplant into my funny body are about as long as the president going on the road with a black and white minstrel show."

"I'm sorry," said Liz. "I really am sorry." The odd thing was that she meant it.

"Hey," said De Witte reproachfully, catching her hand, "this has all got a bit weighty for two people that don't know each other from holes in the wall. Anyway, what do I need a new heart for? The one I've got's still ticking." He released her to feel for his own pulse. "There, what did I tell you? Just needed a bit of intelligent company to cheer it up. Damn doctors, what do they know? There's nothing wrong with my heart that getting out of this place and back to work won't cure."

He sent for some tea. It came in a silver pot, with three cups. He saw Liz counting them. "My wife will be here any time."

She got up from the chair hurriedly, awkwardly. "Is it that time already? Listen, I'll have to go. You don't need me playing gooseberry—" If he had wanted her to go, she had already reasoned, he would not have sent for tea and there would not have been three cups.

De Witte waved a broad hand at her. "Sit down, have your tea. What do you think we do during visiting hours that we need privacy for? I've got a bad heart, remember. Anyway, I want you to meet my wife. Since I've been in here her social circle has narrowed to people in white coats. It'll do her as much good to see a fresh face as it's done me."

If Elinor De Witte was surprised to find her husband entertaining a young woman in his room she showed no sign of it. She came forward with a smile and received De Witte's introduction and abridged explanation with every sign of welcome. Liz, on the other hand, was left wallowing gauchely in the wake of a surprise so total and so badly disguised as to verge upon the uncouth. It was not the fact of De Witte's being married which so startled her—she had not given the matter any thought, it seemed to have no relevance to her task—but the extraordinary beauty of the woman who was his wife.

She was as tall as Liz, thirty years older but still with the strong, slender grace of a gazelle. Her long fine hair had not so much greyed as faded from fair to an indeterminate shade like raw silk, and it was bent up behind her head in a French pleat. She had great grey eyes and skin that more than half a century of strong sun had done nothing to coarsen, had only turned faintly luminous. Liz, who was not unaware of her own physical advantages but had long ago decided they did not matter worth a damn, was mortified to experience a sudden brief pang of envy. Gone almost before she could recognize it for what it was, it nevertheless left her feeling, for the first time, that she had lost control of the situation, become only

another player in her own drama. She struggled
mentally to regain the initiative and wondered if her
composure was as disordered as her concentration.

If it was, Elinor De Witte chose not to notice. She
offered her hand, the long slender fingers cool. "How
do you do?" She spoke with refinement but no affec-
tation, with an almost classically English accent but
one from thirty years ago. "I hope you'll enjoy our
country as much as my husband has obviously en-
joyed your company." It could have been a veiled
cattiness but it patently was not. She was not a
woman who would have chosen to express herself in
that way. Any censure she had to offer would be
conveyed with honesty and dignity, not by means of
a barbed pleasantry. The woman was genuinely glad
to see De Witte cheered by his unexpected visitor.

They had the tea. Mrs. De Witte poured. After
perhaps half an hour it became apparent to Liz that
De Witte was tiring rapidly and soon she would have
to leave. She knew she could return tomorrow, but
those twenty-four hours that would be long to her
would be endless to Joel Grant, frightened, possibly
hurt, in the hands of a violent and dangerous man
who must himself be aware that the risk of entrap-
ment was growing with every minute he spent on
hostile foreign soil. It seemed probable that Grant
could not afford her caution.

Apropos of nothing she snapped her fingers.
"That's where I've heard your name before! Do forgive me," she added, immediately contrite, "but it's
been bothering me ever since I found out you
weren't my Uncle Paul."

"My name?" said De Witte, unconcerned. "You
mustn't believe everything you read in the papers,
especially when they aren't censored."

"There were two men on the plane. They spent

the whole damn journey talking—I think they must
know everyone in the land. When they said De Witte
I listened in for a minute—I didn't know then how
large a tribe it is."

"There are fewer flies on a water buffalo," De
Witte admitted. "What were they saying?"

Liz shrugged. "I don't know, really. I lost interest
when I realized it wasn't Uncle Paul they were talking about. Oh—they mentioned a friend of yours; at
least, I presumed it was a friend. Joel Grant?"

Liz held her breath. De Witte thought for a moment. Then he said, "Never heard of him."

"And someone called Mpani," Liz prompted desperately, hoping her desperation was not showing.

Understanding dawned visibly in De Witte's steel-
coloured eyes. "Yes—now I know. That Grant. My
God, some people have long memories. I've been
made a fool of dozens of times since then."

A few minutes later the nurse came, and Liz left
the De Wittes alone to say good night. Her mind was
bubbling with activity. Her foray into the world of
the spies had been rewarded with two most interesting discoveries. The first was that, clearly, De Witte
had no knowledge of Vanderbilt's operation in England. The second was that the mention of Joel
Grant's name, which had failed to ring the faintest of
bells with De Witte who interrogated him, had sent
Mrs. De Witte starting out of her clear, pale skin.

Chief Inspector Corner had been encountering obscure difficulties all day. The ratio of inquiries per
useful result had risen steadily and now stood at a
personal best if not a track record. It was not as if any
of the London experts he was calling had actually
refused to co-operate: nothing so definite, so easy to
deal with. It was more that they suddenly found

themselves embroiled in incredibly long conversations on other lines, summoned to lengthy and repeated conferences, out to improbably timed meals. If one actually took a call, from compassion or by mistake, he promised to come back with the required information and somehow forgot.

George Corner bore the frustration with equanimity at first—there *were* days like that, God knew he had had enough of them in the past; later with suspicion, finally with the absolute certainty that his investigation was being booby-trapped by some upper-echelon dirty tricks brigade. He made three extremely forthright calls to three extremely senior worthies—known, because of the honours it had pleased Her Majesty to bestow on them, as Call me God, Kindly Call me God and God Calls me God—and two hours later, returning to his office after an abbreviated tea in the cafe opposite with a wife who opened her campaign by asking the waitress to point him out, he found it occupied by a young man in a poplin raincoat. Corner, who tended to look more like a marquee than a mannequin, nevertheless appreciated style in others. He knew that raincoat was not of local origin. London, Paris, Rome, New York possibly; not Manchester. The last idea in the head of the man who tailored it was that it would be useful to keep the wearer from getting wet.

Corner looked pointedly at the name on the door. "Yes, this is mine."

The young man smiled. It was a self-assured, satirical smile as sophisticated as the raincoat. "I took the liberty of waiting for you in here."

"Yes," agreed Corner, "you did."

"It occurred to me you might prefer to conduct our business in private. However, it doesn't matter to me if you leave the door open, switch through the intercom and tune in all the radio cars as well."

Corner shut the door, with restraint. "Who are you?"

The young man flashed the smile again, as if it was something he was famous for. "My name is James."

Chief Inspector Corner was not obtuse, but he did occasionally choose to misunderstand. "All right, Jimmy, suppose you tell me who sent you and what the message is and then we can both get back to doing something useful."

The urbane Mr. James did not much like being addressed as Jimmy. It showed in the tiny frown that gathered between brows so perfectly shaped, so elegantly arched, they might have been plucked. But he did not make an issue of it. He had probably, decided Corner, been called a great deal worse in his time.

"London," James said judiciously, "is a little surprised at the amount of time and effort you feel able to devote to this one case."

"London is." Corner nodded thoughtfully. "What did you do, conduct a Gallup poll?"

James smiled, thinly but not without humour. "Whitehall, if you prefer."

"The Foreign Office? Or something a little more obscure than that?"

"It's not as if," James went on smoothly, "any of those involved, except on the fringes, are British subjects."

"So the Foreign Office—or whatever—thinks I should only concern myself with crimes committed by or upon voters?"

"It's the backwash of somebody else's war. It may be reprehensible of them to continue it on our soil, but they've kept the action by and large between themselves. An English newspaper office was broken into, an English house was entered and an English girl got a bump on the head. That's all that need concern you; and that's pretty small stuff by police standards, surely."

"A man has been kidnapped. There's every reason to believe that he will be taken out of this country by force if"—he paused fractionally—"*London* doesn't pull its finger out and start sending me answers instead of singing telegrams."

"The missing man is a South African. The man who's got him is a South African. They're going back to South Africa, which is where their differences should have been settled in the first place. We have enough home-grown problems: you spend your time on those, Mr. Corner."

George Corner thought for a moment. He hung up his coat and sat down behind his desk. Then he favoured James with a friendly smile. "Tell you what, son. You tell the Grand High Poohbar, or whatever it is your chief calls himself these days, to tell the Foreign Secretary what it is he requires. The Foreign Secretary can make a formal request to the Home Secretary, and the Home Secretary can have a quiet word with the Chief Constable. The Chief Constable will tell my Superintendent and my Superintendent will tell me.

"By which time, almost certainly, either I will have found this big Boer who treats other people's countries like an adventure playground, or the poor bastard who thought he was safe in England will have been dragged beyond the reach of any help I can give him. That will save me having to tell the Superintendent, for the consumption of the Chief Constable, the Home Secretary, the Foreign Secretary and the Grand High Poohbar, that the time to wonder whether Joel Grant was worth protecting was before he was given sanctuary in this country, not when the thug employee of a Fascist government thumbs his nose at our laws and international convention in order to take him back."

Patrick James said quietly, "I understand your anger." The slick urbanity had stripped from him like a veneer as Corner failed to succumb to it. "And yes, you're absolutely right: if we do this through channels it'll take forever. In fact, it won't get done at all, because most of the people in that chain of communication won't put their names to a formal request of that kind. So no, we probably can't stop you doing your job. But we have a good reason for asking you to hold off."

"I find that difficult to believe," Corner said evenly.

"I dare say. But then criminal law—with all its complexities—is like a child's first reader compared with the world of international relations. You know about choosing the lesser of two evils, but what about backing evil men in preference to good ones because in the long run what they can achieve will be of more lasting value than any amount of well-meaning idealism? We have to do that. The bigger the picture, the blacker parts of it are, but we have to work in those areas precisely because that's where the dirt is. It's muck and brass: the dirt is where the power is, and to keep the lid from flying off and the contents hitting the fan we have to find ways of tapping into that power. Yes, we're working with substandard material —Christ, we *are* substandard material! But the alternative is a pristine anarchy.

"Chief Inspector, I'm with you. Joel Grant had a right to expect better of us. He fought against tyranny in his own country for as long as his strength held out, and when he was mentally and physically exhausted he was lucky enough to get out, and to be accepted into a country where tradition, government and law all guarantee equal rights for all citizens. He must have thought he'd died and gone to heaven. He was entitled to suppose he was safe. And then he wakes up one morning to find himself back in the hands of the people he damn nearly died to escape from. We've let the bastard in, we've let him find him, we've let him take him—knowing he'll end up back in Pretoria with his head wired to a triphammer—and now some creep from Whitehall is explaining to the only man standing between him and the abyss why we should let him fall.

"And the reason is this. If you catch the Boer, if you kill him in a showdown, if Grant goes free or if any members of the British public become involved, we have a diplomatic incident on our hands. We have to accuse South Africa, they have to deny it, it'll mean formal protests and recalled ambassadors, it'll probably end in frozen relations and trade sanctions and God knows what else. And that just could be enough to project South Africa into bloody revolution.

"We are almost the last people they respect still having anything like normal contacts with South Africa. There are plenty of decent people who say that's not to our credit. But if we scrape them off our shoes they won't mend their ways: they'll revert to the old Boer fundamentalism of Kruger and Vorster. The liberals won't stand a chance before that bulldozer, but the blacks will turn it on its side. They're not going back; it's only that tiny trend towards liberalization that has kept them from open rebellion so long. If the whites try to turn back the clock it'll happen, overnight. It has to. If the blacks ever plan on being free of Afrikaner oppression it has to be now. The country's a powder-keg: it won't explode,

it'll erupt, and half Africa will be sucked into the fire-
storm. The casualties could run into millions. I'm
talking about the human equivalent of a nuclear
event."

Chief Inspector Corner sat at his desk, regarding
the young man speculatively for rather longer than
might have seemed necessary. Finally he said,
"Sonny, I'm going to do you the courtesy of supposing that you believe all that and further, of supposing
that you care. To me it sounds pretty far-fetched that
the likes of Joel Grant could be the catalyst for an
African Armageddon; but again, I'll accept your
word for it.

"But I have to tell you, it doesn't alter one scrap
the job I have to do. Juggling the fate of nations may
be part of your brief but there's nothing whatever
about it in the police manual. My job is to uphold the
law, here and now, and to protect those who wish to
live within it from those who choose to act outside it.
It is my duty to help Grant to the limit of my ability.
Do you understand that? I have no option; it is my
duty."

"You won't get the help you need to succeed." The
hard edge of frustration on Patrick James's voice was
burred with regret.

"I'd guessed that already."

Liz loitered downstairs, in the hospital's reception
area, waiting for Mrs. De Witte to emerge from the
lift. Her mind was operating, like a sophisticated ro-
tary wing, on two distinct and contra-active levels.
On the lower level her thoughts were in turmoil,
spinning invisibly without drag or lift, dramatic and
useless as a feathered blade. It was crazy enough that
De Witte should know nothing—and he clearly knew
nothing, Liz had been watching very closely and no

one dissembled that well—about the matter she had travelled so far to take up with him, risking her safety every time she opened her mouth; for she had no illusions about the degree of protection her British passport would afford if her prying came to the attention of the authorities. It just meant she would be snatched covertly, after dark, instead of in broad daylight on the public street. If they were prepared to send a man to England in pursuit of Joel Grant, they would not waste a moment's worry on the prospect of pointed questions should Liz Fallon disappear in Pretoria. Indeed, the very fact that she had been allowed to leave De Witte's room and reach unimpeded the public parts of the hospital confirmed that she had been asking the wrong questions, or the wrong person.

But what had really set her mind whirling was the extraordinary way Elinor De Witte had responded to the casual use of Joel's name. If it was clear that De Witte knew nothing of Grant's predicament, it was equally obvious that his wife was aware of Vanderbilt's activities. Liz could conceive of no possible reason for such a paradox; at the same time, the afternoon had been a success in that she now knew where to pursue her inquiries, and Mrs. De Witte might—though only might—be an easier nut to crack than the colonel.

All that was on the lower, roiling level. Immediately above it Liz had battened down a hatch of half-inch pragmatism. She had things to do which she could not allow her confusion to infect. It would be time enough to sort out the implications when she had more facts: right now the important thing was to avoid being sucked into that mental vortex, to where reason would drown, her grip would slacken, her calm detachment vanish utterly, leaving her naked before her enemies. She had still to control the monster, even though it was changing shape visibly in front of her.

When Elinor De Witte emerged from the lift, alone, Liz fell into step beside her. The older woman did not seem surprised. She said nothing, hardly glanced Liz's way; but her profile was strained, drawn in lines of quiet despair. She looked as if she had not slept for a month.

Liz said quietly, "I believe we need to talk"; and after only a moment's hesitation Mrs. De Witte nodded and led the way outside to her car. It was already dark.

5

It was late in the evening when the doorbell rang. Will Hamlin answered it. It was not so much that he had moved into Liz Fallon's house since the drama of Joel Grant's abduction, more that he had not yet got round to going home. He had only returned to his office once, for a couple of hours; he had achieved nothing useful and left. To all intents and purposes Nancy Prescott was running the place, a situation that was a great deal more familiar to her than her employer would have supposed.

Outside it was raining, cold northern rain falling heavily without any need of a wind to make it penetrate. In the meagre shelter afforded by the Victorian porch and lit wanly by its pale lamp was Detective Chief Inspector Corner, clad in a Manchester raincoat whose only virtue was its stubborn impermeability and a late marque trilby.

Hamlin's heart, which was altogether too sensitive

an organ for even a very minor press baron's, skipped a beat and then raced. "News?"

"Of a kind, yes." The policeman sounded dull with fatigue, but something was putting an edge on his voice and he seemed reluctant to meet Hamlin's gaze. "Is Mr. Shola in?"

Wordlessly, Hamlin showed him into the front room.

The table-top was lost under a welter of papers, unwashed cups, an open telephone directory. Nathan Shola had the phone in his hand, about to dial: when he saw Corner he put it down and stood up. "Have you found Joel, Mr. Corner?"

The policeman shook his head.

A muscle at the corner of Shola's mouth tightened abruptly. "Then the bastards have won."

"Not yet," said the chief inspector, "but—" He stopped and took a deep breath. "Look, this isn't easy. I'm here to say something I never expected to have to say, and I'd appreciate being allowed to get it said and leave, because I can think of a dozen good reasons why I shouldn't be here at all."

He went on, picking his words carefully: "It has been made clear to me that, for political reasons which you probably understand better than I, the range of extra-departmental services and facilities I would normally expect to call on and receive in connection with this type of investigation will not be available to me in the search for Joel Grant. Such a withdrawal of co-operation would always be a major handicap: in the circumstances of the present case the scale of it can hardly be overstated. It means, and I am both embarrassed and ashamed to admit it, that I cannot guarantee that every possible effort will be made to secure Mr. Grant's safe release. Indeed, I must tell you plainly that I seriously doubt the ability of my officers, unaided, to find Vanderbilt before he finds an alternative way out of the country, with Grant in tow if that is in fact his intention.

"Mr. Shola, I regret and resent more than I can tell you the fact that persons in positions of authority in this country have made it virtually impossible for me to do my job. In these circumstances, and in contravention of every professional instinct and inclination, I feel I must say to you that you would do well to ignore our earlier conversation, when I asked you to keep your people out of the way of my people. If you have the sort of contacts, among your countrymen in exile or other supporters of your cause, who can help you to find Grant, you should call on them now. You are probably his only chance."

He looked once round the room, located the door behind him with obvious relief. He looked very much older than when he had first come to the house, old and weary and disappointed. He moved stiffly, as if in pain. "I believe, gentlemen, I've said what I had to. I'll go now." He moved stiffly towards the door.

With the fluency of youth and outrage, Will Hamlin intercepted him. "You do realize, Chief Inspector, I'll have this on the front page of every newspaper in the land?"

George Corner regarded him levelly. "I hope you will, Mr. Hamlin. But until then, watch out who you answer doors to. No, forget that," he added, his voice flat, "they don't wait to be asked in. It's the ones you find behind your desk when you've been out of the office that you have to watch for."

Nathan Shola moved out from behind the table he had been using as a desk. In the close confines of a small room he was startlingly tall. "Mr. Corner—before you go. I am grateful for your honesty. I recognize that this situation is not of your making. What I can do I will, and without embarrassing your government if that is possible. Thank you for coming."

After the policeman had gone he sat down again slowly, folding his length into the chair, and Hamlin let out his breath explosively. "The bastards!"

Shola shook his head. "You're spoilt, Will. I tell you, there isn't too much wrong with a state where a senior policeman will sacrifice his career for a man he doesn't know, whose ideals he doesn't espouse and whose presence in his country he probably rather resents."

Like Corner, Hamlin was ashamed, too deeply humiliated to listen to a counsel of conciliation. "When the Home Office gave Joel Grant permission to stay here it accepted a duty to protect him. To deliberately renege on that responsibility is monstrous."

Shola laughed softly. "Will, men like you and Chief Inspector Corner are the keystones of democracy. I doubt you'd last five minutes in my country. But if you did—by God, what a land fit for heroes you'd make there!"

Hamlin could not tell if he was joking. He was not, but he smiled anyway and reached again for the telephone. "All right, I suppose we'd better do something useful with the information Mr. Corner has put his head on the block to give us."

Evening wore into night, and into early morning. The time passed slowly and, for the two men working in the quiet house, wearily; but not without profit. Colombian coffee put on a couple of points on the FT index and British Telecom was assured a dividend for its shareholders. Finally, a little before dawn, Hamlin was startled awake by a hoarse cry from the front room. For a moment he stood confused, unable to recall where he was or what he was doing. Then he recognized the kitchen sink where he had rested his eyes a moment while the kettle filled yet again; probably he had drowsed for only a few minutes, but it was fortunate that the plug was not in place for the kettle had filled and overflowed.

Then he remembered the cry and hastily turning off the tap hurried back to the front room.

Shola was grinning at him, a slash of brilliant white in the dark face. There were black shadows under his eyes, even if they were hard to see.

"You've got something."

"I believe so, yes. You remember the plane at Gatwick?"

"They've moved it?"

"No; no, they're not that stupid. But it finally occurred to someone—it should have been me but it was in fact Tom Savimbe who works at Heathrow—to check on the pilot's activities. And it turns out that two hours ago he received a telephone call at home and immediately left for the airport. He told his wife he was required for a mercy flight with a sick child: I told her I was the anxious father and she was very reassuring. But Gatwick doesn't have him down for a flight of any description. I eventually found him on a flight to Glasgow, travelling as a passenger."

"Glasgow?" Hamlin's tired mind worked at it. "They've got another plane."

"Glasgow has Captain Crane down to take a leased Heron out to Zaire via Cairo with an urgent cargo of mining equipment this morning."

"Christ. How long have we got?"

"Not long enough. All right: where do we get an air taxi?"

Jacob Sithole drove the De Wittes' big car. Liz wondered if it was safe to talk in front of him, but the
thought that it might not be clearly did not occur to
Mrs. De Witte. Liz shrugged off her misgivings: time
was important—for Joel, and also because she could
not risk De Witte's wife having second thoughts
about talking to her. As soon as the car was moving
and the driver at least partly occupied with the traffic, she said, "You know why I'm here, don't you?"

Elinor De Witte nodded her head once, precisely.
She was looking out of the window at the passing city
and made no attempt to meet Liz's gaze. "About
Joel."

"You know him?"

"I've never met him."

"Your husband tortured him within a few inches of
his life but he hardly remembered the name. It
meant much more to you. What do you know about
Joel Grant that Colonel De Witte doesn't?"

"I've known about Joel since before he was born."
Suddenly she was crying, silently, without tears, betrayed only by a slight rhythmic shaking of her narrow shoulders. It was a way of crying for people who
could not afford to be seen crying.

All Liz knew of Grant's childhood was that he had
been born illegitimate, raised poor and more or less
adopted by Joshua Mpani in his early teens. Liz made
a great leap of intuition. She said incredulously, "Joel
is your *son?*"

Elinor De Witte shook her head again, struggling
for control. Her hands were knotted in a cotton lawn
handkerchief, twisting and wringing. "Not mine.
Joachim's. Neither of them knew. Neither of them
ever knew."

The early years of their marriage (said Elinor) had
been hard and idyllic. Elinor worked beside De

Witte as he broke the bright veldt for farmland, and loaded for him as calmly as a duchess on a grouse moor as he fought off raiding parties. At first they thought the hardship and worry were why they were not having children, which both of them wanted passionately. They supposed that when their life settled down a little it would happen.

But after ten years, with Elinor approaching thirty, they were desperate enough to seek help. When the doctor declared there was no physical obstacle to conception they returned to their farm inspired with new hope; and indeed, within six months Elinor's swelling belly was beginning to push out her clothes.

"I was thrilled, of course. Delighted. But Joachim was like a child at Christmas."

They lost the baby. It died before term, and she had to labour to expel the thing with no hope of fulfilment. The hard, long travail damaged her inside and afterwards the doctor said they must not think of trying again. De Witte swore to her it did not matter, and cried like a thing broken when he thought she could not hear.

"Tell me about Joel."

When De Witte was called to Pretoria they were almost middle-aged. It was then that her husband had the only (Elinor said with confidence) fling with another woman in all the years of their married life. It was brief, apparently not very meaningful to either of them, and over by several weeks before Elinor learnt of it—from the girl herself, who arrived on the farmhouse step one day with the two bottom buttons of her cardigan unfastened.

It had not been blackmail which prompted her visit, or vindictiveness, so much as sheer desperation. She had not known when she saw him last, and she had been unable to break through the ring of secu-

rity at his office in order to tell him. She thought he
might have given instructions to keep her at bay
because no one would even take a message. They
took a phone number and said he would call, and he
never did. Finally, thinking he might be at home one
weekend, she got a ride out to his farm, only to be
met by his wife.

"I think she would have left without saying anything, but between what I could see and what I could
guess there wasn't a lot of point. And I wanted to
know."

She was about twenty-two. Elinor could see nothing about her that would have tempted her husband
to adultery after fifteen years, but accepted that she
was not seeing her at her best. She was worried and
frightened, carrying a baby she did not want for a
man she never expected to see again, with no family
of her own to see her through and no money to raise a
child. She was in dire need of help, and by the time
Elinor had prised her story from her and supplied
handkerchiefs and coffee to stem the tears it had
been clear to both women that whatever arrange-
ments needed making would be best made between
themselves.

"I don't remember being shocked, or even terribly
surprised. I felt I should have seen it coming. I wasn't
even angry with her, and I still loved Joachim with
every ounce of my being and believed he loved me
the same way. The thing with Mary Grant had been
an aberration. The more I thought about it, the luck-
ier I felt that she had come to me, not to him. He
would never have left me, but having to choose between his wife and his child would have ripped him
apart."

Elinor provided the money for the girl's confine-
ment. She thought that once the baby was safely

born and the risk of disappointment past, she would adopt it and present Joachim with his child with as much love and pride as if she had borne it herself. But by the time she was ready to leave hospital Mary Grant had become as attached to her baby as mothers usually do. Anticipating—unfairly, in fact—that Elinor's interest in the baby would result in a custody battle she was ill-equipped to win, she discharged herself a day early and disappeared up-country with the new infant in a flight that both must have found tough to survive.

Elinor knew that one word to her husband would have half the security forces in the country searching for his missing son. She did not want to do that, seeing in it the start of a chain of consequences that would destroy them all. Instead, discreetly, she employed a private detective. Whenever he found them she sent money and expressions of friendship, and they hit the road again, trekking the length and breadth of the country in Joel's first year of life. At last Elinor came to see that she was hounding them with her money, sent a final contribution and notice of disengagement, and dismissed the private detective.

For twenty years she heard nothing, did not know if her husband's son was alive or dead. Then the rebel group of Joshua Mpani rose to prominence, and a counter-insurgency measure captured fourteen terrorists including a twenty-one-year-old white boy called Joel Grant. The weeks that followed were the worst of Elinor De Witte's life.

"Should I have told him?—that by keeping Mary's secret I had let his son become a traitor and a terrorist; that the boy whose body and mind he had already mangled and would have to mangle some more was his only child? What could he have done? To help him escape would have been to betray everything he had worked for and believed in. To hand Joel over to someone else would have meant only that his interrogation would have been less efficient, and so longer. I had to spare him that choice. I had to. I lay awake nights praying that the boy would die." She smiled shakily. "I don't know what our minister would have to say about that."

Liz wondered how their minister, or indeed Mrs. De Witte herself, came to terms with the fact that her husband extracted information from people in the same way that a liquidizer extracts juice from vegetables for his living. But she refrained from saying so. She was acutely aware that the answers she had come here seeking were only moments away, and hardly dared breathe for fear of scattering them like startled butterflies. She chose her way and her words with exquisite care.

"Mrs. De Witte, Joel is a friend of mine. He lives in my house in England; I've been helping him get over what happened to him here. It took time because he was hurt badly, but he was beginning to pull his life together again. I think you might have liked one another, at least if you'd kept the conversation off politics. Anyway, I like him. I care about him.

"And then two nights ago a man broke into my house and took my friend away. He was a man from your husband's department, and he appears to be trying to smuggle Joel out of Britain, presumably in order to bring him here. Mrs. De Witte, can you tell me why?"

Elinor De Witte met her eyes for almost the first time since the surprising moment in the hospital room. Her head lifted and her voice was almost steady. There was an unmistakable courage in her demeanour, at once dignified and vulnerable. She said, "I too acted from love. What I did was inexcusable, unforgivable. I knew that at the time. I managed to persuade myself that it was an act of patriotism, that the greatest good of the greatest number was what counted, and that somehow it made a kind of sense of everything that went before—losing the baby, my childlessness, Joachim having a son he didn't know about. That was essential, you see. And he had to live. So many people depending on him—not only me. No, I cannot ask you to forgive me. But try to remember that I did it for love."

"Did what?"

"Afterwards I had this terrible sense of awe. I knew then how wrong it was—even for Joachim, even for love. I tried to stop it, but nobody would listen to me then. I had served my purpose, told them how to save him—they weren't going to turn back because of what they considered my quite irrational sense of guilt. They said I'd get over it when I had Joachim safely home again. And poor Joel was only a terrorist to them, you see, not a son—not nearly a son. I couldn't stop them. Can you? Please, can you?"

"Elinor. What did you do?"

The telephone rang as Hamlin was about to pull the front door closed behind him. He waved an explanation to Shola in the car and trotted back inside.

The line from Pretoria was clear. The tremor was in Liz's voice. "Will, have you found him yet?"

"No. But we have a good lead—we're hopeful. Liz, you have no idea what the police—"

"Will, listen. Tell Nathan. You have to stop this. Somehow you have to. I know what they want him for."

"Shall I call Nathan? He's in the car—"

"Listen." He heard her suck in a deep breath six thousand miles away. "Joachim De Witte is dying. He needs a heart transplant, but they can't find a suitable match. Joel is De Witte's bastard. Will, they don't want Joel at all. They want his heart."

Life for Life

1

Vanderbilt drove to the address he had been given. It was a lock-up garage barely a mile from the airport perimeter, directly under the flight path. It was already dark—another night was setting in—and as he hunted for the right alley the lights of a big passenger jet seemed to fly down the street towards him. Involuntarily he ducked. He knew the thing was already hundreds of feet up and climbing, but human instinct had been bred in before there were aeroplanes.

He picked it up in the rear-view mirror and watched it go with regret. He would have liked to be on it, but once again his plans had been frustrated. When he called his controller back, from a filling station outside Dumfries, he was told that a suitable plane had been located but the earliest departure they had been able to arrange was the following morning. Once more he was faced with killing time in a hostile land surrounded by enemies. He was advised to wait until dark and then make himself at home in the garage. A van would come for them in the morning.

He found the key, and the dust hiding it appeared undisturbed. Still he entered cautiously, checking inside and outside and only driving the car into the garage when he was sure he had neither pursuit nor ambush to contend with. He locked the door behind him and groped around for the light switch.

All down the long side wall were packing-cases, stacked anything up to three deep. Many had been used before and carried old Customs markings. He found one which had already been to Zaire, that carried an old red stencil claiming "Machinery— with care," and pulled it down. It was one of the smaller crates, big enough to take the folded body of an unconscious man but perhaps not big enough to look that it would. The top was loose, and when he removed it the contents made him grin: a hammer, a tin of nails and an enormous suit of overalls. Someone else had picked the crate out too. Joel Grant would enter the airport in the packing-case, as cargo; Vanderbilt would enter in the overalls, as a cargo handler. He would stay aboard after the last crate was loaded and, since he should never have been there at all, would probably never be missed. There would be no difficulty getting himself and his burden off the plane and through Customs at the other end. The Hastings was going beyond Zaire.

He pulled the overalls on over his suit, then turned back to the car. He was still worried about the sedative, unsure whether he should risk using it. The only other option, since Grant had to be kept quiet throughout the loading and right through until the plane was in the air, allowing for any delays, was another fairly substantial thump behind the ear. For a cargo Vanderbilt had been warned to handle with care Grant had already been knocked about a good bit. If Pretoria was right the drug would be safer; if Grant was, the rabbit-chop would be. Finally deciding that if there was to be a débâcle, with a dead body smuggled thousands of miles at massive risk and expense, it would be better on Botha's record than his own, so once again he prepared the hypodermic. He compromised a little by reducing the recommended dosage by twenty per cent in consideration of Grant's frail physical condition and suspect medical history. A bleary mumble in the depths of a packing-case in a cargo plane with the screws already turning was a small and justifiable risk.

Only then did he unlock the boot of the car, unlock the handcuffs, untie the rope anchoring his feet and drag Grant out.

Grant had been confined in the dark, cramped trunk for some hours. The force of the weak, fly-bespeckled light bulb hit him like a blow and above the gag his eyes screwed tight against it. He could not straighten his legs and when Vanderbilt let go of him he crumpled awkwardly to the cement floor. He hardly felt it as in quick succession the hard rough floor hit his knees, elbows and face. He had long since passed the apex of pain to which the cramps had steadily risen and which had had him whining into his gag in the rattling dark while sweat and tears mingled on his temples. Until his circulation returned to normal, inflicting as much agony in the flood as it had in the ebb, all sensation would be dulled. He lay on his side on the floor, eyes clenched against the light, and waited patiently to be picked up.

Vanderbilt looked down at him: not without concern, but it was the concern of a trucker for valuable goods possibly damaged in transit, or a vet for a hamster that might not make it through the night. Professional detachment like an impermeable membrane stood between Grant and any hope of compassion. So when Vanderbilt knelt before him and began chafing vigorously at his sleeping limbs, it was a purely pro-

fessional service, given and received as such. All it
meant to the Boer was the careful handling of fragile
goods; all it meant to Grant was some more pain to
add to that he had already had. He did not see in it
the grains of another escape. He no longer thought in
those terms. He knew he was too weak now to fight
his way out of a wet paper bag.

When he was satisfied with the results of his efforts,
Vanderbilt fastened the handcuffs round his prisoner's left wrist and to the towing-ring under the
bumper. "Sweet dreams," he said.

So passed the third night they had been together,
without incident except for the brief disturbance
that followed from Grant lapsing into an exhausted
slumber and dreaming far from sweetly. Vanderbilt
slapped him awake in a manner oddly similar to the
way Liz used to free him from nightmare, even with
something of the same gentleness.

Vanderbilt had himself and his prisoner ready to
leave before dawn, but it was well into the morning
before he heard the throaty rumble of an engine in
the alley outside. Just in case he knelt by Grant and
folded a hand across his mouth. But at the quiet
rhythmic tattoo at the door he rose to his feet and
went to stand by the door. *"Ja?"* It was too late for
concealment.

"Captain John Crane, Mr. Vanderbilt. I believe you
have a cargo for me."

Vanderbilt opened the door. Captain Crane did
not so much walk in as fly in, propelled from behind
by a large black hand. The other large black hand
held a gun. Towering in the doorway, Nathan Shola
seemed for a moment to represent the quintessential
vengeance of all black men against all white:
Montezuma's revenge, and Atahualpa's, and Cete-
wayo's, and Steve Biko's, and Nelson Mandela's. He

was not so much a man as a vessel for an anger which spanned centuries and continents, a storm of rage contained in glass, visible and potent and constrained only by that flimsiest of fabrics, civilization. In that first moment he could have killed them both, in cold blood and without compunction, as he had killed his enemies when he fought on his own land; and if he had been alone it is probable that he would have done. But he was not alone and he was not at home, and the moment for murder passed; and when it had he followed the gun into the garage and Will Hamlin followed him.

Inevitably, Danny Vanderbilt had faced death before. Not many times: he was too good at his job, and so were the people he dealt with, for that kind of thing to become a habit. But it had happened: the feeling was familiar, that deep dynamic stillness of body and mind that lasted perhaps only a moment before events proceeded, demanding their own responses almost automatically. But afterwards that frozen moment of death in a cage was what he remembered. Sometimes he could not even recall exactly how he had evaded it: his training went as deep as instinct, but no training could wipe out those few glacial moments in his life when he had confronted infinity down a dark tunnel maybe .38 in diameter.

Now here was another one. Staring at the gun in Nathan Shola's hand—not down the barrel, it was not pointed at his head, Shola knew better than to choose the smallest effective target and anyway he did not owe Vanderbilt the favour of a clean kill—he felt the same stillness, the same coolness in the air, the same sense of waiting for history to take its course. He was not afraid, not even of the likelihood of pain. He was irritated, hardly more than that, to be thwarted so close to success. He wondered if there was any way he could take at least one of them with him; Grant, unfortunately, was some distance behind him and certain to remain there, attached to the car and hunched up on the cement floor in front of it.

Vanderbilt looked up from the gun to the face of the man holding it. It was hard enough to drag the eyes away from the organ of his imminent destruction, but it was necessary. Guns never showed weakness. "You, I take it," he said, "are Shola."

Shola's face displayed a black rage seen, as it were, through a veil of watchfulness. It was bad news for Vanderbilt, who would have much preferred a mouthing, spitting fury, lurid threats and a waving gun. There was a small chance of being shot almost accidentally, but the excitable gunman was little more than a dangerous child to be disarmed. Shola was something else: another soldier, another professional. The anger in his eyes would not distort his vision, nor the fury in his soul interfere with his reactions. He would not be hustled into firing off potshots before he was ready, and when he was ready he would hit what he aimed at. Vanderbilt had faced death before: not until now had he felt in the marrow of his bones that the odds were on the other man's side. Had it been a situation where he could have admitted defeat, turned his back and walked away he would have done so. He had no time for death before dishonour. But he knew that if he walked past Shola with his back turned he would not reach the corner of the street.

Shola said, softly, soft and sibilant as the hiss from the lips of a serpent, "And you, I suppose, are the bastard who beats up on women and breaks up sick kids."

"Him?" Vanderbilt had to screw on his heel and look back over his shoulder to see Grant. He did not look sick: a bit the worse for wear, perhaps, but time in a car boot tended to do that to a man. He had had the opportunity to work off the worst of the night's cramps, and the sudden turn in events had filled his body with animation though he could only kneel beside the bumper. The life was back in his eyes, too, which never left Shola's face, although Shola would not glance away from Vanderbilt long enough to return the look. Vanderbilt said, interestedly, "Why, what's wrong with him?"

Shola's lip hardened. "You've had him three days and you don't know? You think he was always scared of the dark? What the hell good would he have been to us? You did that to him—you and your Security Police and your Section Sixes and your twenty-four-hour interrogations. And De Witte. Oh yes: do you know about De Witte?"

Vanderbilt thought he knew all about De Witte. He shrugged. "I don't know what you're talking about. Shell-shocked? He nearly broke my neck. He did kill my pilot. But for that we'd have been out of this country thirty-six hours ago. I wish he had been sick. I wish De Witte had done a proper job on him."

In Shola's eyes the anger surged. He took a long stride forward and swung the gun; the barrel clipped Vanderbilt across the jaw with enough force to send pain lancing through every nerve in his face but not quite enough to fell him. He reeled back, agony pulsing in his skull, taking care to reel towards the car.

Shola stole a moment then to look at Grant. "Joel, my friend, we almost lost you this time."

For Grant reprieve had come almost too abruptly on top of despair. His face was aglow, his eyes bright with fever and unshed tears. He could hardly speak; all he could do was repeat, "Jesus, Nat; oh Jesus," and fret at his chain like a dog.

"Easy, Joel. We'll have that thing off you in a minute. First, tell me has he got a gun."

On his knees by the bumper, Grant looked up at the big Boer. Vanderbilt had one hand on the car wing to steady himself, only partly for the sake of appearances, while the other nursed his raging jaw. Behind hooded eyelids he was hoping that he had not miscalculated, that the pain would not prove too much of a disability. He was hardly aware of Grant's burning gaze.

Grant said unsteadily, "He was taking me back to Pretoria." It was not possible to tell whether the tremor in his voice was due to fear, or hatred, or only deep fatigue, all of which cast their shadows by turns across his hollow face.

Shola spoke to him sharply. "The gun, Joel. Did he have a gun?"

Without shifting his gaze Grant responded. His voice was strange, strained. At first he seemed to be talking at random, talking out the horror. Only after a minute did Shola realize that it was a reply of sorts; not an answer so much as an invalidation of the question. He said, "He was going to take me back. To De Witte. To have my head ripped up again. I fought him, Nat; I did fight him, but I couldn't beat him. I couldn't even make him kill me. But I got the pilot."

Vanderbilt waited for the pause, as if unwilling to interrupt him, and then said quietly, "There is a gun. In the car, in the glove compartment. He never saw it."

Shola despatched Will Hamlin with a jerk of his head. Hamlin kept carefully clear of the line of fire and went to the nearside door: the Boer was beside the driver's door. The pilot, Crane, was at the back of the lock-up—not because he hoped to find an exit there but because it was the furthest he could get from the gun. If he once knew how far a hand gun can throw lead accurately, given a good enough hand, he was trying hard not to remember. Hamlin took Vanderbilt's gun—a little gun, not much more than a lady's gun, that would disappear in his big hand but still blow incapacitating holes through anyone who stood in his way—and returned with it, holding it gingerly, the way he had come.

Shola said, "Now the keys. Free him."

Grant said, still in the same oddly flat voice, "He's good, Nat. They knew what they were doing when they sent him. He may be better than you. You should kill him now. Before he finds a way to fight back. You should kill him now. For what he's done. For what he was going to do. Kill him, Nat. Kill him now. Or let me do it."

Vanderbilt had taken the keys to the handcuffs out of an inner pocket and was bending towards the kneeling man. He stopped then and turned his gaze towards Shola, quizzically. "I gave you my gun," he reminded him gently, with the mildest possible reproach.

"Yes," agreed Shola.

"I won't go on being helpful if you're going to shoot me for my trouble."

"I know how to unlock a pair of handcuffs."

Will Hamlin was looking between them, one to the other, with increasing anxiety. He could not tell if they were serious. He knew Grant was, but Grant could be forgiven. He did not know Vanderbilt, only by his works and reputation, but Shola he had known long enough and well enough to know he was capable of it. Despite the lightness of his manner, he thought Vanderbilt knew that as well. He cleared his throat. "Er—I'll whistle up the cavalry, shall I?"

Without sparing him a glance, Shola said, "No."

Vanderbilt sighed. Bending again, fitting the key to the lock where the cuff braceletted the towing-ring, he remarked to Grant, "I don't suppose I'd have liked the prisons here any more than you liked ours."

"I think here they keep the electricity for running the television sets," Grant said.

Vanderbilt smiled. "How quaint."

Hamlin was oblivious of the small exchange. All his attention was focused on Shola. His voice was low, vibrant with urgency. "Nathan, we have to get the police. Somebody has to drive these bastards away in a Black Maria."

"The police aren't interested. They washed their hands of it, remember? Well, we managed without them and we sure as hell don't need them now. You want to do something useful, you could call up a hearse."

Hamlin shook his head quickly. His heart was pounding. He counted Shola his friend. They espoused the same causes: Hamlin fought for them with words, Shola with weapons. Hamlin had never challenged his right to wage war for the freedom of his own people in their own land. But now, for the first time clearly, he perceived the true nature of that commitment. There was nothing intellectual about it. It was to do, only and always, with hatred and with blood.

Will Hamlin had carried the strange device that was a reasoned peace in Southern Africa long after sensible people had taken sides or arranged to be elsewhere for the duration, but it had never seemed utterly impossible until now. The reason was the four other people in that dusty Glasgow lock-up. Not one of them wanted peace. They did not want compromises and accommodations. They all wanted total victory.

This was not exactly news to Hamlin. He had known of course that the old Boers would sooner raze the country than share it, and he knew there were black leaders who felt the same way. Still he had persisted in believing in a middle-ground that was more than a dream of weary men and idealists; had thought that a commonality existed to be tapped in intelligent people on both sides. He expected to be disappointed by men like Vanderbilt, but the discovery that his intelligent, articulate friend was no more interested in just settlements than Pretoria was turned his heart to ice. In that moment all his hopes, the gentle breeze that had kept flying his banner with its strange device, sank and died. He recognized that he had been wrong.

But the idea, if unattainable, was still right; and, stubborn in his own way as were the others in theirs, he was not prepared to stand by while murder sullied it. He took a deep breath and tried to hold his voice steady. "Nathan, you're not going to shoot them. I won't permit it."

For almost the first time Shola took his eyes off Vanderbilt. "You won't?" His eyes were filled in complex patterns and proportions with anger, hatred, hunter, menace and a tiny bewilderment. Probably instinctively his gun rounded with his gaze, settling briefly on Hamlin's belly.

The ice in Hamlin's heart spread, a numbing grief. His voice broke. "Nathan—"

Movement on the periphery of his vision brought Shola's eye and gun racing back to the car, but it was already too late. Vanderbilt had used the scant distraction to yank Grant to his feet by the short chain and held him now before him like a shield, his fettered wrist twisted up his back, the chain kept taut by the large hand which gripped his shoulder, the strong blunt fingertips digging into his throat. Still captive despite the taunting proximity of freedom, he was dragged unceremoniously backwards as Vanderbilt hastened to put the steel plates of the car as well as the body of his hostage between Shola and himself. Even as he did so his right hand was inside his coat. It came out taloned with a five-inch blade that winked broadly in the dusty light. "He never saw this either," he observed by way of an addendum. He was hardly breathing any faster.

Grant's teeth parted in an inarticulate cry of rage, frustration and soul-deep despair that brought erect, like soldiers, every hackle. The howl ripped from him until Vanderbilt's hard fingers choked it off. "That's better," murmured the Boer.

After a single murderous glance at Hamlin that burned his face like acid, Shola was back behind his gun, sighting down the length of his arm at what remained of his target. He said, very coldly, "Unless you let him go now I will shoot bits off you until you have nothing left to hold him with."

Vanderbilt chuckled appreciatively. "You may be that good," he allowed. "Some people are. A lot more just think they are. Precision shooting requires constant practice, and I don't think you've had that sort of spare time. You'll hit Grant a dozen times before you find me."

"You want to risk that?"

"Certainly. I'll go further: I'll give you one free shot, after which we'll decide what we're going to do. After all, if he's dead then—"

"Or if you are." Shola let the gun drop slightly, caught his falling right hand in the rising palm of his left and pushed the blunt muzzle back up. His feet planted wide and his square stance gave him as steady an aim as he could contrive. There was no perceptible movement of arm, hand or weapon. Still wearing his Amsterdam suit, he was an ebony statue of a fighting man.

Hamlin said, "Nathan."

"Damn you, stay out of this," Shola grunted. "I can do it."

"You can kill Joel."

"So? Knowing what this is about, do you really think that matters? If it's the only way I can stop them leaving, I'll kill them both."

"It isn't. Nathan, it isn't the only way." Hamlin's voice nagged away with the uninspiring message of common sense. "All you have to do is keep them here for five minutes while I get help. Five minutes, Nathan, and it can all be over."

"It can all be over in two seconds. I don't want your government setting up deals and sending him back to Pretoria. He deserves to die."

"Probably. But Joel doesn't deserve to be sacrificed, not to De Witte's well-being and not to your vengeance. Nathan, we haven't come this far so that you and not Pretoria can be his executioner. For pity's sake—if you don't care what I think, wonder how you're going to explain it to Liz!"

For a long moment Shola continued sighting down the brief barrel, all his body tense with concentration. Then, slowly, the tension leaching away, he sucked in a deep breath and raised his head. "Go get help."

"Excuse me," said Vanderbilt, "I'm very sorry but I can't agree to that."

Shola's mobile lip lifted. "What the hell do I care what you agree to? While I have the gun you're not leaving this garage."

"And while I have the knife," Vanderbilt said, almost apologetically, "neither is your friend. Unless he wants to come back to a charnel-house."

"Go," Shola said tersely. Hamlin took an uncertain step towards the open door. Vanderbilt calmly placed the point of the blade below Grant's right eye and drew the razor-edge firmly downwards. Blood sprang all the length of the wound from cheekbone to jawbone. Breath hissed in Grant's teeth and his eyes rolled. For a moment his knees seemed to buckle; Vanderbilt held him up by his chained arm.

Hamlin's eyes stretched wide with horror; and underneath the horror was the sick realization that such barbarism was new and shocking only to him. There were large parts of the world, and the three other protagonists (the pilot was a mere spectator) all came from one of them, where brutality he could hardly imagine was stock-in-trade. Hamlin had known that, had cared enough to try and fight it, but he knew now that knowing and caring and fighting at an intellectual level and actually being there, seeing and maybe suffering and having to cope with the brutality were two different things. He felt he had somehow wandered into the wrong world. He felt like an impostor, as if everything he had tried to do with the *Democrat* was based on fiction and hypocrisy. He wondered fleetingly how he had the gall to criticize Shola's kill-while-the-killing's-good barbarism when barbarity was so clearly the coinage in use and he himself had no answer to it. He recognized, with grief and shame, that if Shola had come to this rendezvous alone Vanderbilt would now be dead and Grant safe. He swayed on the spot, unwilling to stay, unable to leave.

Shola grated at him, "Go, Will. Go now. Don't look back."

He tried. He turned away and took a couple of

resolute strides towards the door; but the hiss of breath like an almost silent scream made him falter and stop, and he turned round, his eyes drawn to the quiet horror as if by a magnet. Blood was washing down Grant's face from a second cut, a perfect parallel to the first. "Jesus Christ."

"Damn you, Will," snarled Shola, "get out of here. He's carving him up for your benefit. He'll stop when you're gone."

"I won't, you know," Vanderbilt said pleasantly. "When there's no one between me and my plane—that's when I'll stop."

"Dream, Boer." Shola's gun was still sighted on the scant bits of Vanderbilt showing behind Grant's head. His arms were beginning to ache, but while there was a chance that the big man would make a mistake and show enough of himself to present a target Shola was not going to lose a bead it could take him half a second to find again. Half a second was all he would get.

"Of course," Vanderbilt went on conversationally, "he might run out of face before that. I thought I'd move on to his eyes then. How about that, sonny?" He jerked on the chain. "You reckon you'll be much use to your friends with no eyes?"

Grant mumbled something, indistinctly because he was trying not to use his cheek muscles.

"Sorry, what?" said Vanderbilt, jangling the links again.

"I said," Joel Grant gritted through his teeth, "I haven't been much use to them since last time I played silly buggers with you people, but I have to tell you I'm quite getting the taste for it again."

Shola stared at him in a kind of wonder. Vanderbilt chuckled, almost paternally. "I told you there wasn't too much wrong with him. Mind you, that was five minutes ago."

Deep in Hamlin's brain, where shock had not wrapped all the gears in cotton wool, it occurred to him to wonder whether the big, humorous man who had come so far and risked so much to return Grant to his native land actually knew what he was wanted there for. He thought it might be useful to find out. "And how much use do you think he'll be to Pretoria if you blind him?"

"That is a point," Vanderbilt conceded. "I'd better leave him one eye, just in case. And his tongue. Otherwise, you'd be surprised just how much of the human body can be dispensed with at need." It was true: if Vanderbilt's briefing precluded him from practising vivisection on Grant, there was no way Grant's friends could be sure of that.

But Hamlin said softly, "You don't know why they want him, do you? You don't *know*—you've been storming through my country, leaving a trail of blood and damaged lives, and you don't even know why."

Vanderbilt said patiently, "I told him, and now I'll tell you, and maybe after that I won't have to say it again. I don't have to know. All I have to know is what they want me to do, and then do it. Which is why, when my plane leaves, I shall be on it and so will as much of this boy as is left. It really would be best if you went home now."

"Over my dead body," Grant said deliberately.

"Hush, sonny," Vanderbilt said quietly, "the grown-ups are talking."

Grant ignored him. "I'm serious, Nat. You don't owe me much, but you owe me better than to leave me alive with this man."

Hamlin looked at the harrowed, bloody face, appalled, unaware that he was hardly more prepossessing a sight himself with his horror-smitten eyes staring out of the utter pallor of exhaustion. "What does he mean?"

Shola said nothing.

"I mean," said Grant, thumping home the emphasis, "there's more than one bullet in that gun. Shoot us both if you have to, I'll take my chance. I don't care about dying. But don't leave me with him. Don't let him take me back."

Shola made his decision abruptly and acted on it immediately. He dropped his left hand from under the gun and moved quickly backwards until, outstretched, it found Hamlin. "Go. Go now, and go fast."

The strong black hand launched him at the door. Hamlin went. He was out of the garage before Vanderbilt's blade was halfway down Grant's cheek a third time.

2

Vanderbilt sighed and moved the knife away from Grant's face and under the angle of his jaw where the carotid artery throbbed. He remarked to Shola, "I don't suppose I'll impress you with a blood-show, will I?"

"I've seen it before."

"Yes. The next person who comes through the door, I cut the boy's throat."

"You'll be dead before he is."

"Yes, possibly. Well, that's the game we play."

There were a few moments of silence. Then Shola said thoughtfully, "If my friend Will was still here he would say there was an alternative."

"Would he?"

"He would say that if you let me take Joel, and I let you and your flying friend there take your aeroplane, we could all sleep in our own beds tonight."

A slow grin spread across Vanderbilt's broad face. "Your friend Will doesn't really understand about people like us, does he? He doesn't appreciate that if I go home and leave Grant here alive I'll never work again; and that if you let me go back, having once had me in your sights, none of those who now look up to you will ever again trust your judgement or accept your authority. He doesn't realize that we're both fighting for our lives here, or that if either of us cared more about the future of our children than the fates of our ancestors there would be no problem in South Africa. We can't resolve the dilemma: we are the dilemma."

Slowly Shola returned the smile. "Maybe after you and I are dead—?"

"Perhaps." For a tiny space of time the nearest thing to empathy of which the two men were capable dwelt on the air between them like a shimmering bubble. They were still enemies, always enemies; but they also had more in common with one another than either had with anyone else. Vanderbilt pricked the bubble. "But I rather doubt it."

Someone began laughing. It was a thin sound, not entirely without hysteria but laced with a real if arcane humour. Shola and Vanderbilt exchanged a puzzled look before they realized it was Grant. His face was turned away and the blood from the wounds on his cheek had washed over his jaw and down the side of his throat, and his narrow shoulders shook with improbable laughter.

Vanderbilt jerked on the chain. It had become a means of communication for him, a way of focusing attention. If he remembered that every time he did it he came closer to dislocating a man's shoulder, it did not trouble him. "What's amusing you then?"

Pain had become an inane chorus for Grant, a kind of meaningless intermezzo. At regular intervals throughout the performance the orchestra would strike up and he would be hurt again; but it did not mean anything. He could think through it now. His thin reedy chuckle broke for a moment on a caught breath, then resumed a note lower. Then he said distinctly, "Joel Grant—game for a laugh." But neither Shola nor Vanderbilt spent much time watching English television, so the allusion eluded them, leaving them more mystified than before.

A minute passed. Shola said, "You realize Hamlin will be back with the police any moment."

Vanderbilt nodded, apparently unconcerned. "And you know it won't change anything. Except that there'll be a messy trial instead of a tidy funeral. I'll still kill Grant before anyone can reach me, however many there are. The only difference is they won't let you kill me afterwards."

Shola said, with hard conviction, "You really think they can stop me?"

Vanderbilt shrugged. He looked at the door behind Shola, he looked briefly at the blank wall behind himself and the roof above him, and he sighed. He said, "I don't suppose it would do any good to tell you there's a friend of mine behind you with a gun."

The slow, arrogant smile spread Shola's lips. "None," he said, and the man behind him swung his gun, clubbing Shola into black oblivion.

Vanderbilt remarked, "I don't know who you are, but I think I was safe describing you as a friend."

Patrick James said quietly, "I shouldn't count on it." He knelt quickly beside Shola, twisting the weapon out of his limp grasp and transferring it to the pocket of his poplin raincoat. He thumbed open Shola's eyes and touched his rather delicate fingers to the pulse along his throat. He straightened up, unconsciously brushing dust from his sleeve. "Well, he won't be bothering us for a while."

"What about the other one?"

"I hit him too."

Vanderbilt regarded the young man curiously. He was around Grant's age, slight like Grant—although it sat better on him: he looked naturally gracile rather than half-starved—and also not tall. Vanderbilt, who had in his own mind only recently graduated from the ranks of the Young Guard, suddenly felt middle-aged, and that his world was being overrun by children with guns. He sniffed. "Well, if you're not my friend, and you're clearly not his friend, whose friend are you?"

James looked at the big man, still almost hidden behind his prisoner. They had not met before, but he recognized those features he could see from photographs: the corn-coloured hair, the very blue eyes, the breadth of the shoulders, the big butcher's hand swallowing the knife. There was, he decided, enough of Pretoria's gorilla showing to present a marksman with three or four adequate targets. Two of them he was sure he could hit from here, snap shooting with a gun as tolerant of imprecision as a rocket launch. He also knew what would happen if he did. He vented a world-weary sigh. "I'm nobody's friend. I'm just here to try and prevent wars."

Vanderbilt nodded sagely. "I can see that wouldn't make you popular."

James managed a tired smile. Neither George Corner, who had been too angry and disbelieving to study him in detail, nor Danny Vanderbilt, who was too far away and unwilling to move closer, had seen the shadow in his eyes of the weight that hung on his soul. He was a young man, but already he had carried it too long. There were too many occasions in the course of his job when he had to do things he did not like, and he strongly suspected that this was going to be another. Also, it was getting to be a long time since he slept. A battery shaver in the glove compartment of his car had kept his young man's smooth face fresh, but he knew of no similar placebo for the gnarled and cynic spirit it hid. Afterwards he would drink too much wine and fix himself up with a girl who would not notice if he kept forgetting her name, but before that he had to resolve this situation. There were several possibilities, but his instructions tied at least one hand behind his back. He supposed Vanderbilt had the same problem.

He said, "How are we going to get you out of here before you stop being a nuisance and start being a diplomatic disaster area?"

Vanderbilt sounded genuinely apologetic. "I am a reasonable man. It embarrasses me that I am not at liberty to agree to a reasonable compromise. I would like to be able to leave Grant here, get on my aeroplane and go home. I think you would find that acceptable?" He paused for confirmation and James nodded. "But I can't. My briefing was specific: to bring Grant back to Pretoria if at all possible, or to kill him here. If I cannot take him aboard our plane I must kill him, and then you must—well, do as your briefing tells you. A bullet in the head or a trial at the Old Bailey: either way I'm afraid I'm going to go on being a nuisance. No reasonable compromise is possible. I am sorry."

"Mm, quite." James considered for a moment. "Have you ever thought about getting out of the game? Now would be a good time. I can provide you with asylum, with cover if you want it, probably with an income. Think about it: people like us tend to find it difficult to retire in our own countries, and you won't want to be still doing this when you're sixty."

"Defect? To a country with a climate like this?"

"I could throw in a sun bed."

The muscles of Vanderbilt's shoulders were beginning to protest. He had been holding Grant in this awkward position, intermittently taking most of his weight, for several minutes now—precious minutes, that should have seen him on his way to the airport with his cargo carefully crated in the back of Crane's van. While the pilot was trapped here too there was little risk of the plane leaving without him, but a long delay could start the questions coming. Getting himself and Grant on board unnoticed depended on no one paying more than the routine minimum of attention to the loading and clearance procedures. So while there was any possibility that he might get out of the garage with his prisoner, there was an element of urgency.

He said, "Which lot are you with?"

"One of the lots which don't exist."

"Ah—you too. Where do you work to—Whitehall?"

"Whitehall would wet itself if it even knew about my lot. I don't imagine you have the same problem with Pretoria."

"No indeed, Pretoria is very proud of us. Until we get caught *in flagrante delicto* in other people's countries, of course. Because then they have to rattle a lot of sabres and stir up a lot of ill-will to camouflage the fact that we had no business being there in the first place. They'll be downright annoyed with me if it comes to that. But they'll also be cancelling all leave for the armed forces."

"There's no need for it." The urgency was also beginning to show in James's voice. "Leave Grant and go home. No one need be any the wiser. Tell them he's dead: I'll put out the same story, we'll relocate him, give him a new identity. Not for your sake, or mine, or even his, but because of the effect a diplomatic engagement now will have in South Africa. You can't afford any more destabilization. You're living in one giant gas leak: you don't need somebody to strike a match. It was a bad briefing. De Witte would never have given it—would he? In all the circumstances you're doing your country a disservice by trying to carry it out."

He broke off, frowning. Vanderbilt was beaming broadly at him, as though someone had just dealt him the last ace.

"I know who you are," said Vanderbilt. "You're one of Carver's army."

"Does it matter who I am?" James rasped testily.

"It does to me, sonny." Vanderbilt was grinning as if he could not stop. "We know about Carver. He gets the best, and he makes damn sure they stay that way. You don't carry that gun for hitting people with. You practise most days and you're accurate to—well, over this sort of range, single atoms. If you'd been prepared to shoot me you'd have done it when you walked in here. Shola would have done it, if he'd been good enough. But he thought he'd hit Grant. You, on the other hand, have been told that getting Grant back is of only secondary importance beside getting me off British soil. They don't want me here, dead or alive. So the gun is a bluff. You might as well put it away. I'm leaving here with my prisoner and my pilot, and if you stick around you'll probably hear my plane."

He moved out from behind the car, straightening,

pushing Grant before him. Six inches bigger all
round, he presented all the target anyone could
want. It made no difference. James sighed and returned his gun to its holster. Vanderbilt had done
better than guessing at his orders: he had known
what they had to be. There was nothing more he
could do. He saw the pilot still cowering uncertainly
and sent him after Vanderbilt with a weary nod of his
head.

He heard the van outside start but it did not move
off. Instead Vanderbilt came back into the garage
alone. James thought rapidly about his gun, saw no
point in drawing it and left it where it was. Vanderbilt smiled an avuncular approval, as if he knew everything that passed through the younger man's
head. Perhaps he did. They were very alike.

He said, "Can't go without this," and went to lift
the packing-case. He was a strong man but it was an
awkward shape. He looked slyly at James. "On the
basis of 'If it were done when 'tis done, then 'twere
well it were done quickly,' you wouldn't care to give
me a hand with this thing?"

James replied quietly. "I don't know how or when,
but sometime there'll be an account to pay for what
I've had to do today."

Vanderbilt met his cool grey gaze without surprise
or disdain. "I know." He bent his back to the heavy
crate and staggered outside with it, unaided.

Will Hamlin lay rather than sat against the brick wall
of the alley, nursing his broken forearm and trying to
get his head together. He was aware of the purring
that was the van's engine without at first appreciating its significance.

He had left the garage like a rugby forward with
possession. In his right hand was the small gun that

he had taken from the glove compartment of Vanderbilt's car, that he had not so much hung onto as never got round to parting with. He was barely conscious of it; certainly in his hand it did not constitute a weapon. He sped from the garage, down the alley and sharp right where it turned towards the road.

Patrick James had been half a stride behind Shola all the way. He too had thought to check on the pilot, had followed him to Glasgow and found the Hastings, only to have one of the ground crew say he had missed the captain by moments and point out the blue van in which he was driving away with two other men, one of them black. Without the time to hire transport he acquired a car by flashing an impressive but quite illegitimate card and shouting "Police!" at its owner, and set off in a pursuit that was both hot and covert.

He trailed the van to the alleyway. There was a sign advising it was a dead end, so he parked the borrowed car and continued carefully on foot. From the vantage of the corner, unsuspected by men wrapped up in their own drama, he heard most of what was said and saw Joel Grant almost become a free man before being snatched back into captivity. He knew then what would happen, and what his own part must be. When Hamlin came sprinting round the corner, gravel spitting from under his shoes, James was ready for him.

He knocked the forgotten gun from his hand with the axe-blow of his own barrel that broke his arm. Hamlin went down, the shock getting him behind the knees and keeping his legs from coping with his own momentum, and rolled wildly, helpless to protect his damaged arm. When he fetched up against the wall James kicked him soundly in the jaw. Then he calmly pocketed the little gun and walked towards the garage.

Now Hamlin was coming back. He had been unconscious for some minutes and he was not really ready to wake up yet, but the new sound of the engine was striking chords of compulsion in his aching brain even though he was not yet up to remembering why. Exploring slowly, he discovered that his right arm was painful, weak and creaking nastily, and that all the teeth in his left jaw were raging. He pushed himself up against the wall and almost passed out again.

But through his own hurts the throb of the engine beat insistently. He knew it was important, and when he made himself think he knew why. It meant somebody was getting ready to leave. If Shola had won it was him and Grant getting out before the arrival of the police they believed were on their way. But if Vanderbilt had won Shola was down or dead, and Grant was on the penultimate leg of his last journey. If it was Shola all was well: they would stop for him or the police would pick him up, he was not too bothered which. But the man who hit him, whom Hamlin remembered only as sudden unexpected movement and an explosion of pain, would have altered the balance of power in the garage. Hamlin began the long, arduous climb to his feet.

Vanderbilt was behind the wheel. The pilot was in the passenger seat. Grant was in the crate, in the back, bound, gagged and finally drugged. While Vanderbilt was nailing the lid on he had contrived to beat repeatedly on the slats with some mobile part of his anatomy, but the noise had quickly grown faint and now there was silence. Grant was sliding down a midnight velvet tunnel into deep unconsciousness.

Just as the Boer had at last yielded to the need for

it, so in the end Grant had fought the needle. Vanderbilt threw him like a roped calf in the back of the van, face down, stapled his instep over Grant's elbow and shoved the hypodermic in to half its length. Then he lifted Grant bodily and tossed him into the crate and hammered the lid down.

He had by no means discounted the possibility that when they prised the top off they would find only a corpse, stiff and shrunken, diminished to a doll without the nervous energy which had animated it. He hardly cared. He had done his job; if someone else, Botha or his medical adviser, had proved unequal to his, Vanderbilt would find it hard to regret that their mistake had saved Joel Grant from another encounter with his monsters. All Vanderbilt wanted now was to be home.

When the van rounded the corner Will Hamlin was in the middle of the alley, on his feet but only approximately vertical, swaying slightly as if there was a breeze. He looked less like a running forward than an old boxer who has taken too many punches. Neither to left nor right of him was there room for the van to pass. Vanderbilt sighed and trod gently on the brake.

"No!" It was the man beside him, who had led these people to him, who had cowered in a corner of the garage all the time he might have been trying to atone for that, who now considered the moment opportune to reassert himself. "Run him down. Run him down! We can't afford any more time." His voice was harsh and excited, and if he had been driving he would have done it. Vanderbilt hoped he would keep a cooler head about any emergencies which arose at thirty thousand feet.

The van coasted to a halt with its bumper a hand's span from Hamlin's knees. He hardly seemed to see it. He would not have jumped aside if it had come at him; perhaps he could not have done. Only a feat of will was keeping him on his feet.

Vanderbilt pushed back the door and swung down. Hamlin let him walk right up to him before he even raised his head, and then it was an effort. His face was haggard, his eyes dull with pain. Vanderbilt said gently, "You'll have to move, you know."

Hamlin cranked his head a little higher to look him in the eye. "You have no right—"

"No," agreed Vanderbilt. "None at all. But I'm taking him just the same. Will you move?"

Hamlin shook his head, mute and stubborn. Vanderbilt laid a hand quite lightly on his broken forearm, cradled in front of him, and Hamlin's knees gave under him. The Boer caught him as he dropped and put him back against the wall. But before he could straighten up Hamlin fisted his good hand in Vanderbilt's sleeve, letting the other trail on the ground like a bird's broken wing. Vanderbilt hung onto his patience: hitting an injured man was about as good for his ego as beating girls. "Let go."

Hamlin's voice was a hoarse whisper, thick with hurting and desperation. "You don't know why they want him."

"I told you, I don't have to know. All I have to do is take him back."

"They don't care about anything he knows or anything he's done. They want his heart. They want to transplant his heart into De Witte. Joel Grant is De Witte's son."

As if he had not heard Vanderbilt broke the frail grasp of Hamlin's clutching fingers, returned to the van and drove away.

3

Liz Fallon, wearing her prettiest dress, walked
quickly through the reception area towards the lifts,
exchanging smiling nods with the people on the desk
as she did so. They knew she was visiting their VIP.
There had been some discussion about her, over the
teacups. Some of them believed she was De Witte's
mistress, brought in to cheer him up now that he was
dying (had not a queen of England once made such a
gesture out of love for her dying king?) but the more
worldly among the women pointed to her clothes
and expressed the opinion that London was the devil
of a long way to bring a mistress and he was bound to
have one closer.

Liz had the lift to herself, so she let the smile slip. It
was inappropriate to both the occasion and her feelings about it. As the car climbed she was thinking
about Elinor.

By a careful cocktail of truth and suggestion she
had succeeded in reassuring Mrs. De Witte that the
operation would not go ahead. She told her about
Joel's friends in England who were already hard on
Vanderbilt's heels and would undoubtedly pin him
down within hours. She told her about the police who
would be pulling out all the stops, and the careful
check that would be mounted on airports and docks.
She had managed to convey a supreme confidence
that Vanderbilt would be stopped and his prisoner
freed at, if not before, the point where he tried to
escape the country.

She had not said what she already knew, that the
police were being deliberately hampered for political reasons; and when she was called from an early

lunch by the telephone, and it was Will Hamlin
phoning from hospital in Glasgow, his voice thick
with pain and defeat, while the doctors hovered irritably in the background waiting to anaesthetize him
and set his arm, she felt no compulsion to pass on to
Elinor the bitter news he brought her. Nor was there
anyone else whose help she could call on. The possibility she had foreseen when she bought her plane
ticket had finally developed: Grant's last hope was a
friend on the ground in Pretoria.

She had not, in all honesty, expected to be able to
free him. She had considered the pros and cons of
launching a public scandal, but decided it would take
a great deal more in the way of atrocity, and a great
deal more time than she would be allowed, to mobi-
lize public opinion in this three-monkeys of a city.
She had come reluctantly to the conclusion that the
best service she might be capable of doing Grant,
who had lived in her house and slept in her bed and
shared his worst dreams with her, was to contrive his
death before he disappeared again into the bowels of
the building where they had wrecked him before.

But what she had learned from Elinor De Witte
altered things, raised the possibility of new solutions.
True, the likeliest end was still death or imprison-
ment for both Grant and herself, but there was at
least a chance for them if she was successful now. She
dared anticipate success. The foundations for it had
already been laid. But she took no pleasure in it, did
not relish—even apart from its implications for herself—what she was about to do.

The lift doors opened and she cranked the smile
back into place, and stood for a moment chatting and
joking with the guards of the man she was going to
murder. Then one of them opened the door for her
and, smiling, she passed inside.

She closed the door quietly and turned to the bed, the tiny, utterly serious gun from her pretty purse in her hand. De Witte's grin of welcome died on his lips.

Liz's voice was low and flat, her eyes emptied of emotion; or almost. De Witte saw no fear there, no hesitation, but he thought he saw regret. Liz said, "If you give me the chance I'll explain this. But if you call for help I will kill you immediately and take the consequences. All in all, I don't think your government will want to put me on trial, in open court."

For De Witte the threat of death had been a dark companion for as long as he could remember. He had been within moments and inches of it on many occasions. For more than a year, apparently, it had been only the thickness of a worn heart wall away. He did not wish to die but death held no terrors for him, so he did not panic at the sight of the small, serious gun but took her at her word. "So explain."

Liz drew a deep breath, wondering where to begin. The chain of events had been forged a quarter of a century before, the vital link that made sense of all the rest closed only hours before. Not knowing how far she would get before circumstances forced her to cut short the account, she began with what was, from De Witte's point of view, the most important part. "You have a son."

She told him the story Elinor had told her, about the girl and her child, and how everything his wife had done was out of love for him. Liz knew it was important for him to hear that; it was also, less explicably, important to her that he should know.

De Witte listened without interrupting, at first with disbelief, then with gathering tears brightening his eyes. Liz watched a whole lexicon of emotions play across his white face: grief and anger and delight and regret and shame and hope. And she knew, leav-

ing the difficult parts till last, that he had deeper
wells of feeling yet to plumb.

When she paused for breath, De Witte said, "I
want to meet him. You know where he is, don't you? I
want you to bring him here."

"You've already met him. His name is Joel."

His brow furrowed as he tried to remember. Liz
saw understanding strike him with the force of a
blow. "Joel Grant?" he whispered, stricken. "Oh
dear God."

"Yes," she agreed.

"Why didn't he *tell* me?" De Witte's voice actually
broke.

"He didn't know. He still doesn't. The only people
who ever knew were his mother and your wife, and
Mary died when he was a boy. Joshua Mpani as good
as raised him."

"That Kaffir! Raised my son a traitor?"

"And lost his own life rescuing him from your tor-
turers. You'd have torn him apart but for Mpani. Between you, you damn nearly destroyed him. And
now he's in terrible danger again, and I think maybe
I'm the only person in the world who can help him,
and the only way I can see to do it is with this." She
waved the little gun, and if there was resolve in the
gesture there was also despair.

"You want to kill me? I don't understand."

"I don't want to kill you, Colonel. Perhaps I should
but I don't. But Joel needs you dead. Your people
have him. A man called Vanderbilt kidnapped him
from my house three nights ago, and an hour ago I
heard he'd succeeded in getting Joel out of the UK.
He'll be here tomorrow. And if you're still alive when
he arrives, your people will kill him. Not for anything
he's done, or anything he is except that he's your son.

"They knew about him long before I did. They

have his medical records, from when you had him before and probably from the hospital where he was born. Your funny blood, Colonel—Joel has it too. That's why they want him. They want to give you his heart."

The silence between them grew and stretched and crawled, like a wakening beast. It was as if the monstrous thing was something quick and vital, and in the room with them, stirring and hungering. As if afraid to draw it, neither spoke.

De Witte was a sick man, and the news the woman had brought him had shocked him to the depths of his soul—much more than the gun she was pointing at him. But he was also an intelligent man, and neither sickness nor shock had made him foolish. He had probably as much skill as any man living at determining truth from falsehood: the fact that this was personal did not alter the criteria for judging it.

He recognized the essential truth in what Liz had told him. It made sense, it fitted with known facts, it matched with rational patterns of behaviour; it had the ring not only of authenticity but of inevitability that true stories have. That being so there was no point in launching a barrage of questions that would obscure rather than clarify the basic dilemma. They had almost nothing left to say to one another.

Except: "Joel is still alive?" De Witte was amazed and even faintly amused at the speed with which he had learnt to say his son's name with proprietorial overtones.

"Yes. He has to be, for the transplant to succeed."

"I won't permit it. I can protect him."

"Do you really believe that?"

De Witte thought for a long moment. Then he shook his head. Then he looked up and fixed Liz with a fierce gaze. "Who's done this to us?"

"You'd know better than I," said Liz.

De Witte nodded. "Botha. Not Vanderbilt: Danny would have come to me if he'd got wind of what they were planning. Harry Keppler, of course—my doctor, I've known him since we were boys, he was always a ruthless bastard. The rest of his team?"

"Not necessarily."

"No. Once they have him here and they're ready to go, all it takes is someone to inflict the kind of head injuries transplant donors always have, he's admitted as a road accident victim, complete with forged consents, and nobody's any the wiser. Me least of all. I didn't know I had a son to lose." He sucked in a deep, painful breath. "But Elinor knew. It was her idea, wasn't it?"

Liz saw no point in denying what was self-evident. "Yes. In a desperate moment she confided in your doctor. Afterwards she tried to stop it but they wouldn't listen. She told me in the hope that I could stop it. I think, in the back of her mind, she knew then what I would have to do."

"Kill me."

"I don't know what they'll do then. They know there are people in England who know the whole story. They may give Joel back as the price of our silence. Or they may try to kill us all. If they win I shall die a murderer; but if we win, your death will have bought Joel's life. I can't offer you much in the way of consolation, but I promise that if there's any way at all I'll make sure he knows that. You two were never much good for one another before; maybe—" She did not finish the thought: it seemed impertinent to.

She raised the gun in both her hands. De Witte could see right into the barrel, so she was aiming at his right eye. At least she was not going to make a bollocks of it.

But then, she was not going to do it at all if he could prevent her. He said quietly, "Liz, wait. There's a better way."

"Better for whom?"

"Oh, for you." He added sharply, "I listened to you, girl, now do me the courtesy of listening to me."

"There may not be much time. If someone comes—"

"We don't need much. Just long enough for you to be seen leaving the building. Have you your passport on you? Then forget about your luggage, go straight to the airport and get on the first plane going anywhere. With luck they won't even think about you until you're out of the country. Even if they do pick you up, all they can do is ask you what we talked about. Half Pretoria will know I shot myself after you left."

"Shot—yourself?" Liz's weapon wavered off target as she struggled to comprehend what he was saying.

"You heard."

"You want my gun?"

"No, thank you," he said politely, pulling a cannon from beneath the bedclothes, "I have my own."

She regarded it with that supreme calm which is the only possible alternative to panic in certain extreme situations. Eventually she remembered to breathe. "How long have you had that thing pointing at me?"

De Witte raked up a small smirk of professional pride. "Since about five seconds after you pointed yours at me."

Liz closed her eyes for a moment, trying to marshal her thoughts. She felt her firm, desperate grip on events beginning to slide. She felt that if she lost

control now she would never wrest it back, the chaos
would come pouring in and drown her. She looked
from his gun to hers. It was trembling slightly. It had
come to feel very large—not heavy, particularly,
though perhaps heavier than it looked, but cumbrous
and awkward and out of place. It was not part of her
style, pointing guns at sick old men in hospital beds.
She wished she could put it away. She wished she
knew what De Witte was thinking.

She said, "Let me get this straight. You think I'm
going to put this thing back in my bag, say a fond
farewell to your bodyguard and walk out of here,
trusting in your word as a gentleman that once I am
clear of the building and thus beyond suspicion you
will put a bullet in your own brain?"

"That's about it," agreed De Witte.

"Do I look stupid?" demanded Liz.

"No. Up till now you haven't acted stupidly, either;
rashly perhaps, but not stupidly. Don't spoil it now."

"I've come six thousand miles to kill you!"

"You came six thousand miles to save my son.
There's a difference. You achieved your aim when
you told me who he is. You don't need to risk yourself
any further. There's nothing you can do now that I
can't do better."

"I don't believe you."

"Yes you do. Because if I'd wanted you dead, I
wouldn't have shown you this"—he waved the big
gun negligently—"I'd have used it."

"Then I don't trust you. Joel Grant is your last
chance. Without his heart you'll be dead within
weeks. Knowing what you should do and doing it are
two different things: I don't know what I'd do, so how
can I trust you? Once I'm out of this room and on my
way home, what's to stop you having second

thoughts? It's not as if you have to do anything. All you have to do is nothing, and you live."

"And my son dies."

"You don't know him. You've only met to exchange hatreds and hurts. You wouldn't like him if you could meet again."

De Witte smiled, a shade wanly. "How many fathers do like their sons? How many sons like their fathers? Infanticide is still frowned on in polite society."

"This isn't a joke," cried Liz, indecision and frustration tormenting her.

"No, it isn't. It's my son's life we're talking about. I gave him that life and knew nothing about it. Two years ago I came close to killing him, still unknowing; I would have killed him, eventually, without the intervention of that damned Kaffir who was there for him when I wasn't. You don't get too many second chances in this world, girl, but I've got one now: to give my son life again, and to know it and pleasure in it like fathers are supposed to, and all it's going to cost me is a few weeks of sickness I can do well enough without anyway."

Against all her inclinations, Liz found herself trusting him. She believed he would kill himself in the hope of saving his son, and to save her the consequences of doing it. But once she left the room there would be no going back. She would have chanced her own life on his sincerity, but to chance Joel's she needed to be more than sure.

She said, subtly persuasive, "You could have his life. You could be well again. He was never a son you could be proud of: not only a traitor to his blood but a deserter from his cause. I'm fond of him, but even I don't think he'll ever amount to anything."

De Witte regarded her at once sternly and with

kindness. "If I didn't know what you were doing I'd tell you to stop being disgusting and go away. As it is I'll just tell you to go away. Now. Please?"

She went. She went unsteadily, her emotions tearing her both ways, her mind that had been so sure and determined now a maelstrom of conflicts, an upheaval. She believed he would keep his word, but the awesome responsibility of having thrust that on him, coupled with the implosive anticlimax that came of tooling up, actually and psychologically, to execute a terrible deed only to have it taken from her at the last moment, had left her in a kind of shock, reeling and uncertain. She fumbled the little gun back into her purse and groped for the door.

"Liz!" De Witte hissed after her, and when she forced herself to face him he smiled and said, "Bravely."

She took his meaning. Her head came up, her back straightened and she went out of the room with a quick smile for his guards. Before the door closed between them De Witte called to her, in a marvellously ordinary voice, "And if you do see him again, Liz, give him my love."

She nodded without looking back and walked quickly to the lift.

The lift dropped slowly and the entrance hall was full of people cutting her off from the day. She smiled and nodded automatically at anyone who looked her way. She felt to be moving in a trance. At every moment she anticipated outcry behind her.

The bright day beyond the glass doors restored her equilibrium somewhat. She stood in the afternoon sun, taking deep breaths of the warm scented air and pushing the freshness into the bottom of her lungs. Then she looked up.

His room was at the front of the building, on the

top floor. She did not know which window. They all looked alike, bright and blank as idiot eyes in front of no soul, impervious of tragedy and triumph alike. There was no way of knowing what, if anything, was happening behind them.

For perhaps two minutes she wrestled with the fear that he would go back on his word, and with the urge to return and find out what was happening. If he chose not to die, perhaps believing that he could bully those around him into abandoning their monstrous ambition, choosing to ignore the reality that all the oaths in the world would not stop them slipping him a Micky Finn with his medication and acting in accord with their own and his best interests rather than his expressed wishes, De Witte would not be to blame—she would. She had held his fate, and Grant's, in the palm of her hand, and there was no escaping the fact that—however good the reasons, however plausible the promises—she had left De Witte alive when only his death offered any hope of saving Joel.

But in the deepest recesses of her soul she still trusted him; and anyway it was too late to go back. If he had betrayed her there were men seeking her now; if he had not she risked wasting his generosity by hanging around here. She raised a hand to hail a taxi.

As she climbed in she heard, far above her head, a faint heavy report, muffled by glass, as if someone had slammed a door. She did not look up. She told the driver to take her to Johannesburg, to the airport. Long before she got there the tears were splashing on her hands folded in her lap, and she did not know for whom she wept.

4

When the Hastings was clear of British airspace Vanderbilt vented a long, deeply sincere sigh of relief. And immediately began to feel badly about the whole messy operation.

If he was honest with himself, which was something Vanderbilt tried to be, it was not any of the specific actions which had been required of him that was causing this bad taste in his mouth. There was none he had not done before, without compunction or regret. He wished he had a rand for every time he had used his strength against people who were not his physical equal: women, men, kids, the hurt, the bound, the frightened. None of it was novel, and while he derived no great pleasure from it he accepted the need for it to be done and the desirability of it being done efficiently. Nor was it the first time his success had been crowned by another man's death.

If he was honest, what rankled most was the trail of disorder he had left behind him. Good operations were swift and smooth, and after the mechanic had gone home all that was left to show he had been was the body of his mark, or the burning building, or the empty file where important papers used to be. A good mechanic did not attract attention to himself. Vanderbilt was troubled, and indeed ashamed, that he had left a trail Shola could follow, and deeply bothered that he would not even have won the success that confounds criticism but for the intervention of some smooth-faced ruthless little commando from Carver's army who, except for a fluke of politics, would have been against him rather than with him.

Yet when he reviewed the thing objectively he could not see where or how he should have acted differently.

He shrugged off his seat-belt and edged out into the aisle. There were only a few rows of seats immediately behind the bulkhead; all the space in the central fuselage was filled with crates. They were stamped for Egypt and for Zaire, but one of them was going further. Vanderbilt slouched down the aisle, the seats on either side brushing his thighs, to where they had parked the smallish crate loaded at the last minute from the van.

The flight engineer had noticed and asked what it was; the pilot had told him spare parts. The engineer had gone up to the flight-deck without comment, but he had not appeared greatly surprised by either the last-minute crate or the unexpected supercargo in overalls. If he did not know Kane was working something on the side he guessed; either he was paid off or he genuinely did not care. Vanderbilt made no enquiries: the crew was Kane's responsibility, if he wanted to go on flying he had presumably safeguarded himself as far as they were concerned.

They had left the last crate accessible, abutting the aisle and with nothing on top of it. Vanderbilt stood for a while looking down at it, his hands in his pockets. Then he looked round for something to use as a crowbar and prised the lid off.

Grant lay on his side, curled round, with his knees drawn up. He made no response to the sudden light. He was deeply unconscious. Vanderbilt, wondering leaned closer. Grant's breathing was deep and even, and under his jaw the pulse was firm and steady. He was sleeping, not dying. Pretoria had been right and Grant wrong. And Vanderbilt had been wrong not to use the hypodermic back at the cottage. He would have been home by now if he had, and Piet the helicopter pilot would have gone home to his wife.

Vanderbilt went on gazing at the man in the crate, thinking about what the man with the broken arm had said. That was the reason for that sudden, extraordinary flash of recognition he had experienced: something of the expression, something of the personality of the big old man floating like a mirage in the thin pale face of his sleeping child.

And if that much was true, the rest probably was too. It explained what he had been unable to understand before, how a defunct terrorist could be of sufficient value after two years out in the cold to be worth risking an international furore over. It also explained that odd emphasis Botha had placed on his captive's health. Looking down at Grant's passive, ambiguous face he wondered what terrible divisions in a family could result in a man and his son taking up arms against each other; and worse than arms. Vanderbilt knew what had been done to Joel Grant in his father's house, and he believed Will Hamlin's murmured, fainting accusation. The man had been too tired and confused to lie, his allegation too terrible to be other than true.

He waited for some feeling about that to come and none did. Feelings were not really his line of business. All that he could get his mind round was that Joachim De Witte was his chief, for whom he had untold respect and no small affection, and that Joel Grant was not. He realized that made him an emotional bankrupt, and found he had no strong feelings about that either.

He wandered over to a window. The Hastings was at height and over sea. He wandered up to the flight-deck. The engineer looked at him incuriously, the co-pilot did not even turn round. When Kane saw him he waved him brusquely back. Vanderbilt shrugged and walked back down the plane. A couple of minutes later the pilot joined him.

"Listen, you'd better stay away from those two. They've been paid off, but I'd just as soon they never knew what they've been paid off for."

"All right," Vanderbilt said mildly.

"I mean, Christ Almighty, it's not like a box of rifles or illicit currency, is it?"

"No," agreed Vanderbilt.

"Hell, we all got in the way of carrying extras when they started that sanctions nonsense over Rhodesia, but washing machines and televisions is one thing and people is another, and people being taken somewhere they don't want to go is a different thing again, right?"

"Quite so," Vanderbilt agreed smoothly, bridling his irritation but not so closely that Kane should not catch a dangerous glimpse of it. "Which is why you were not expected to help us out of the mere goodness of your heart." As he said it he winced. There were a number of expressions he was going to have to foreswear after this, because of their loaded meanings.

Kane, who had not been close enough to hear what Hamlin said, did not notice. Nervousness was enough to make him argumentative. "Oh yes, I'm sure it seems a hell of a lot of money to you. But you take out of it the extra fuel, landing charges, sweeteners for those two up front, ditto for people on the ground, and it stops looking quite so generous. And then it may have to last me a very long time, if I can't go home. . . ."

"Not go back? What are you talking about?"

"That fiasco in the garage! Bloody hell, if I'd known to expect that I'd have wanted a damn sight more."

"All part of life's rich pageant," murmured Vanderbilt.

"Your life, maybe. I get all the excitement I need wondering how many of the warning lights on a dashboard are serious. My point is, we left witnesses back there. The black and the kid you were so careful to drive round, they asked for me at the airport by name. They don't just know what I am, they know who I am. So one of them's got a sore head and the other a broken arm: so what? If I take this crate back at the end of the week, I'm going to find policemen lining the runway like landing lights."

Vanderbilt said patiently, "I think you missed the point. The third man, who dealt with the other two. He was from the British government."

"So?"

"So Whitehall—or whoever—is not going to connive actively at our success and then tell the world about it at a trial. They've already made the bed they want to lie in. We were lucky—for their own reasons, they wanted us to succeed. The case was closed the moment we took off, and Jack Carver will make sure it stays closed. If anyone tries to lean on you, let him know—a message left with Special Branch will find him. I don't know how he plans to muzzle Shola and his friend—some judicious blend of threats and blackmail, I would imagine—but that's his problem and unless he's gone off badly he'll handle it. Until this is ancient history, they won't even risk charging you with speeding. What you're going back to is a charmed life."

Kane, who had been studiously avoiding the small crate behind them with its lid off, finally let his gaze settle on it. "And what's he going back to?"

Vanderbilt looked directly at him. "Do you really want to know?"

After a moment the pilot looked away. "No."

"Then don't ask."

Turning back to the flight-deck, Kane glanced at his watch. "We'll be into Cairo before eight. That's where we'll stop over. There's a hotel quite handy but I imagine you'll stay on board. Tomorrow it's a nine-hour haul to Kinshasa and another six to Johannesburg."

Vanderbilt did not require to be instructed in his work, but he was too appalled to resent it. "Two days?" He had flown up by jetliner in fourteen hours, Johannesburg to London.

"What do you think this is," Kane asked blandly, "Concorde?"

Left alone, Vanderbilt fumed silently with disappointment and frustration. Another night—and by then Grant would be awake. He would have to be drugged again: there were risks in that but it was too dangerous to keep him awake. At Cairo and at Kinshasa there would be men on board who owed Vanderbilt nothing, whose sympathies for the most part would be firmly with his prisoner: if Grant was in a state to ask for help he might very well get it. Even in the air he could not afford a scene, if Kane's crew were something of an unknown quantity. Men who would cheerfully turn a blind eye to smuggled goods for the right price might feel very differently about taking a condemned man to his death. It would be far better if they never suspected Grant's presence, let alone his destiny. Still trying to be honest with himself, Vanderbilt admitted that at least part of his reluctance to let Grant wake was because, now he knew what it was all about, he did not want to have to talk to him again. Anyway, he was too tired.

Time and miles passed in the humming aircraft plugging down the sky. They ate a late lunch from a briefcase full of sandwiches and boiled a kettle for tea. The crew ate together and Vanderbilt ate alone, obscurely troubled by the fact that there were five men on board but only four mugs. It was as if Grant was already dead and they were taking his corpse home. For the very first time and only in passing, chasing the thought out of his mind before it could roost, Vanderbilt wondered if he could go through with this.

Over the Mediterranean Vanderbilt took the top off the crate again. Grant was still asleep, curled foetally in the bottom of the box, dried blood under his face from his cut cheek, but this time he reacted to the light, his eyelids flickering, twisting his head away with a little protesting groan. Vanderbilt watched him for some moments, head on one side. Then he grasped the far side of the crate, braced his foot on the rim nearest him and tipped the thing over, spilling its contents into the aisle.

Grant was aware in the dimmest way possible of stirring consciousness. He was aware of the splash of light on his shut lids, and the flaccid painless tumbling of his eviction. He felt the cold and wet as Vanderbilt bathed his face and throat with a soaked towel. He felt himself hoisted by strong hands and walked mechanically up and down. When a mug of water was pressed to his lips he drank. When a hypodermic needle was pressed into his vein he slept again.

At Cairo, after the cargo handlers had finished and the crew had retired to their hotel, Vanderbilt left Grant sleeping on the floor beside his crate, handcuffed to an anchorpoint though the chances of him taking advantage of the concession seemed minimal, and walked up to the flight-deck.

Kane had found a quiet spot to park the Hastings.

The nearest lights were barely sufficient to show it was there, quite inadequate to pick up any movement on board, and Vanderbilt left the cabin lights off. He found the radio by touch and began searching through its bands for something useful. Mostly he would have liked to hear from Pretoria, but that was still most of a continent away and he could not pick up anything he recognized. At length he found an English language news programme and listened to that.

It was not that he expected to hear his exploit discussed. Indeed, with so many interests vested in keeping it quiet it would be an appalling blunder if it became public knowledge. But on a personal level Vanderbilt did not much care. If they would wait another day the world's press could discuss it to their hearts' content, up to and including how he was beaten up by an unarmed, bound and barefoot boy, and he would not care at all. The radio was less for information than for company: for reassurance that a world beyond his trials with Grant continued to exist and was only waiting for him to get home and hand over his prisoner before welcoming him back into its bosom.

He listened for fifteen minutes to a woman discoursing knowledgeably on the Benin bronzes, interrupted at regular intervals by a reporter who clearly thought they had holes in them and sat in public parks between the war memorials and the swings, and then he switched off.

He switched on again an hour later to hear a man saying, ". . . fought in the Western Desert during the Second World War. He took part in many historic actions, and led the now famous raid. . . ."

Vanderbilt had been listening with half an ear for

two or three minutes before he realized that what he was listening to was Joachim De Witte's obituary.

It took him half an hour to find a telephone he could use, and longer to get the call placed. When he finally got through to his office Botha was not there. He had gone home. (De Witte had never left the office while there was anything resembling a crisis on. More than once the nights he had snatched sleep on the little folding cot by his desk had stretched into weeks.)

At least Botha did not have to be roused from his bed. He had taken the phone almost before Vanderbilt had finished giving his name.

"Vanderbilt, where in God's name are you?"

Vanderbilt told him.

"You should have been here yesterday! What in hell went wrong?"

"Just about everything. It tends to, when you're working on your own in somebody else's country. You know?" Botha did not, of course, and Vanderbilt knew it, which is why he said it. "It's all right now, though. We'll be in tomorrow—no, today. This evening. That's not why I called. De Witte: is it true he's dead?"

"You're damn right it's true. The department's a madhouse. I need you back here, Vanderbilt." Botha sounded at once tired and fraught.

"What happened?"

There was the briefest of pauses. "He was shot. At the hospital."

"By who?"

"We're working on that."

"You didn't catch anyone? Surely to God he was guarded?"

Botha always responded to criticism with bluster. "When you show some signs of being able to carry

out your own duties with efficiency and on schedule,
I might be interested in your views on how I should
perform mine. In the meantime the most useful
thing you can do is get back here with that bloody
boy. Though precisely what I'm meant to do—" He
stopped abruptly.

Vanderbilt said deliberately, "You never did explain what we needed Grant for."

Botha responded tartly. "I never considered it necessary to do so."

"Consider it now," suggested Vanderbilt quietly.

"When you get back," Botha promised, "you and I
are going to have a little chat."

"I worked for the colonel for eight years and never
questioned his judgement once. I'm sorry I have to
question yours so soon, but I'm doing nothing more
until I get an answer."

Vanderbilt could picture his chief's round, rather
pasty face flooding with colour, but after another of
those brief pauses he got his answer. "He's a ter. He
never retired from terrorist activity, he's just been
directing it from a safe distance. We think it was his
people murdered De Witte. We think a period of
interrogation will confirm this."

Vanderbilt did not doubt it. Periods of interrogation in Pretoria had confirmed much stranger things.

After he had taken his leave of Botha he thought
for several minutes. Then he rang his office back and
spoke to the duty officer.

"I've just been talking to Botha. That's bad news
about the colonel. Hard to believe he'd take that way
out."

The voice at the other end of Africa was glum,
depressed. "I know. But there's no other way to read
it, Danny. You've got to remember, he's been a sick
man. He wasn't getting any better."

Vanderbilt returned to the parked aircraft, taking pains to remain unseen more from habit than strict necessity. He checked with his torch but Grant had hardly stirred. Then he switched it off and sat in the dark, listening to the soft steady rain of pieces falling into place and forming a picture he did not want to look at.

The dawn came with its familiar celerity. One of the things which irritated Vanderbilt on his excursions into the temperate zones was the lethargy of daybreaks and nightfalls, as if the matter was subject to a twice-daily poll, with recounts. Equally irritating was the way the people of such regions insisted there was something pleasant and desirable in those murky joyless hours bracketing the day like dreary bookends.

In the wake of the quick North African dawn came Kane, striding hurriedly across the tarmac, agitation in every line of his long, angular body. He let himself into the aircraft, calling Vanderbilt's name although Vanderbilt was only feet away, in the last row of seats where the leg-room was greater. Grant was back in the crate.

"What's the matter with you?" Vanderbilt asked calmly.

Kane glanced at him with hunted eyes. "You know a man called Botha?"

Hairs pricked up along the back of Vanderbilt's neck. "How do you know that name?"

"He phoned me this morning. Early, at the hotel. He said he was your boss. Is he?"

"Probably." Vanderbilt's tone contained some irony. His eyes remained wary.

"He wants us to scrub Kinshasa, to fly direct to Johannesburg."

"Does he indeed?"

"There's no problem as far as fuel goes, and I can drop the Zaire shipment off on my way home."

"That's all right, then."

"You're happy enough with that?" Kane sounded relieved, as if he had expected—had been led to expect—difficulties.

"Why shouldn't I be happy? I'm getting home so much the sooner."

"Right. Exactly." The pilot essayed a game if overgenerous grin and went on up to the flight-deck, moving more easily as if the weight lifted from his mind had been a physical burden. Five minutes later the second officer and flight engineer came aboard too. They just about nodded at Vanderbilt, still sprawling in his seat, and he raised a languid hand by way of response. They too disappeared into the nose.

Behind the amiable bland face and the lazy wave Vanderbilt was thinking, with intensity and speed: not so much of the chain of events which had brought him here but of the people whose lives were joined by strange, enduring linkages into that chain.

Of Botha, devious and carping, a man of infinite guile and no greatness, whose rule would be untempered now by the prospect of De Witte returning to claim his desk and file his understudy away where he would be harmless.

Of the English girl, the naked girl he had seen only once, and her calm faith in Grant.

Of Grant himself, still an enigma, an eternal hung Christ pierced through at intervals by the sharpness of other people's ambitions.

Of the black man who could have saved him except that the urbane, ubiquitous civilization of the corrupt old world into which he had come had slid into his soul unnoticed and stayed his hand when a moment of African strength would have ended the thing.

Of the white man, by no standards a warrior, who should have been finished four times over by a broken arm but fought back the pain long enough to deliver his piece of the picture that finally made sense of all the bits that would not fit.

Of the young man from Carver's army and his unattractive proposition.

But mostly of De Witte. De Witte had always inspired a fierce loyalty and genuine affection in his officers, and in return had supported and protected them to the best of his considerable ability. He was one of the last—perhaps the last—of a dying race of giants. Behind the amiable bland face Vanderbilt was grieving for him.

He wondered how much he had known. That they wanted to give him a new heart, probably: he would have welcomed a new lease of life. But that that heart belonged to a living, viable man? Vanderbilt did not believe that De Witte would have sanctioned it. It had the particularly nose-curling stink of Botha's brand of ruthlessness. De Witte was ruthless too but not like that, never like that. And when he found out, certainly about the heart and probably about the donor too, he stopped it. He stopped it dead.

One by one the four Bristol engines broke into life, the propellers turning at first as if hand-cranked, only afterwards dissolving into a blur of their own speed. The ageing aeroplane, like a dowager in a bathchair, trundled past the buildings towards the runway. This early in the morning there was no queue: the tower directed the Hastings to the top end of the runway. Like a dowager pushed by an athletic footman the plane taxied downwind and turned her face back briefly towards the Mediterranean. Kane put on his brakes, made his final checks and ran his engines up.

Under cover of the burgeoning sound and vibration, Vanderbilt threw open the passenger door in the big hatchway. He kicked the crate over, dragging Grant—somnolent, mumbling—out mostly by his hair. He cast sharp glances forward and aft, but no one was watching: the tower was half a mile ahead and on the blind side. Grant's hands were finally free: Vanderbilt used one to haul him to the door and manhandle him through it, lowering his limp body some of the several feet to the tarmac. When he let go Grant dropped inert, a shapeless heap on the ground dressed in another man's clothes stained with another man's blood.

The engine noise dropped back to a lower, throatier rumble. The aeroplane strained for the sky. Either unaware of the open door or deliberately ignoring it, Kane snapped the brakes off.

As the aircraft took that first abrupt stride towards freedom, the dowager suddenly lifting her skirts and bounding from her chair like a sprinter, Vanderbilt finally cast his vote. He followed his prisoner out of the hatch, hit the ground face down and rolled over once, and the broad expanse of the tailplane rushed over his head.

About the author

Jo Bannister, a successful writer and newspaper editor in Northern Ireland, has won several awards for journalism in the United Kingdom, including the Royal Society of Arts bronze medal. MOSAIC is her second novel for the Crime Club (it follows *Striving with Gods*).